WALK
with an
ANGEL

OTHER BOOKS AND BOOKS ON CASSETTE
BY DAN YATES:

Angels Don't Knock

Just Call Me an Angel

Angels to the Rescue

An Angel in the Family

It Takes an Angel

An Angel's Christmas

Angel on Vacation

An Angel in Time

Eyes of an Angel

Lack of Evidence

WALK
with an
ANGEL

a novel

DAN YATES

Covenant Communications, Inc.

Printed in Canada
First Printing: January 2004

10 09 08 07 06 05 04   10 9 8 7 6 5 4 3 2 1

ISBN 1-59156-386-0

CHAPTER 1

Tanner Nelson glanced nervously at his watch. "This will never do," he yelled at the cabbie. "I have a plane to catch, and precious little time to spare."

"Blimey!" the cabbie retorted, shaking his head. "Why the devil must you Americans always be in such a hurry? It's not like I wanted the bloomin' engine to stall." For the third time the cabbie twisted the key, allowing the starter to grind with no more success than the previous two tries.

Tanner exhaled disgustedly. "Can you at least call me another cab? I need to get to the airport."

"Sorry, mate. Radio's on the blink. There's a call box just up the block, so you can call one from there. And let's not be forgetting the six pounds you owe me for motoring you this far."

Tanner grabbed his luggage and climbed out of the cab. Removing a ten-dollar bill from his wallet, he handed it to the man. "All I have is American money, but this should more than cover the ten blocks you brought me."

Tanner backed up a step as the cabbie muttered an obscenity under his breath while grinding the engine again. "Blinking lot you've got to worry about, catching a flight when another will be slipping out just behind. This motor car represents me means of feeding the kids and the missus." The starter ground to a halt, and the cabbie slammed a fist against the wheel. "It's flipping soup we'll be eating tonight, you can believe."

Tanner rolled his eyes and pulled out another five, which he shoved into the cabbie's shirt pocket. Not waiting for a response, he headed off into the fog. At the first intersection, he checked his watch and weighed his options. No way could he catch his flight now. Oh well, he'd just have to make do. There were other flights, just as the cabbie had observed. Noticing a bus stop at the corner, Tanner abandoned the idea of another taxi and took a seat on the bench.

There was something about a foggy London morning that always fascinated Tanner. Fog was a rarity for a native of the Arizona desert. The heaviness of the air felt almost eerie; even the faintest sounds carried through it. The whistle of a bobby directing traffic two or three blocks away reached Tanner's ears with striking clarity. Somewhere off in the distance a dog barked, and footsteps from a pair of leather-soled shoes sounded, hidden deep in the cloudy folds. A feeling of melancholy enveloped Tanner, and for some reason his thoughts turned to Brandon Cheney. The thought of his old friend eventually brought a smile, but he still wondered how a foggy London morning could possibly initiate thoughts of an old desert rat like Brandon Cheney. As always, memories of Brandon came with bittersweet sentiment.

During their college years, Tanner and Brandon were two of a group some dubbed "The Five Musketeers"—a fitting title considering the closeness of this fivesome. It was a running joke that they were too close to even cast individual shadows. The others in the group were Vincent Wagner, Cory Harper, and Troy Adams.

It wasn't surprising that all five should fall in love with the same woman, and what a woman Katherine Dalton was. Beautiful, beautiful Katherine. But in the end, it worked out so not one of them ever won Katherine's heart. Tanner was never completely sure, but he always felt he was the front-runner in Katherine's book. He might have fared even better with her if it weren't for his incessant anxiety of commitment. But the "what if" surrounding Katherine was one page of history that could never be verified this late in the game. One thing he knew for sure—he was still in love with her, just as was Vincent. The rest of them? Well, that was another story, much of which centered around poor Brandon's untimely fate. As for Katherine, she had moved halfway around the world to Melbourne, Australia, and had never been heard from since.

Tanner allowed his thoughts to wander back to the big party held the night after he and the others had graduated with honors from the

University of Northern Arizona at Flagstaff. The party was Vincent's idea, of course. Vincent was the only one who could afford such a bash, and he had access to his father's mountain cabin located only half an hour away from the university. Zachary Wagner was both owner and CEO of Wagner Aerospace, Incorporated. Zachary used the cabin on occasion to entertain celebrities, mostly politicians whom he wanted to charm for business reasons. At Vincent's request, his father made the cabin available for the party. The entire graduating class was invited, about 150 people.

All five musketeers had offered to escort Katherine that night, but it was Tanner who drew the honor. He was never sure if it was him or his car that won her over, since she needed a ride home to Mesa later in the evening, but it didn't matter. What did matter was that she was his date for the night—a night filled with events that flowed back so vividly now.

* * *

"Looks like we're the last ones to arrive," Katherine said as they entered the room where the party was already in full swing. "It's my fault. Sorry I made you wait while I went back to my apartment to tell everyone good-bye. They're such great friends."

Tanner shrugged. "Hey, no big deal, Katie. Even with Cory's appetite, there's enough food left to stock a mom-and-pop market."

Truthfully, it wasn't food Tanner was concerned about; it was keeping Katherine to himself with those four hungry-eyed cowboys just waiting to cut him off at the pass. He had something very special in mind for the night, and had even bought a ring for the occasion. It was a scary thought, but something he had managed to talk himself into. He wanted to wait for just the right moment, and since he would be driving her home, the two of them would be alone. He hoped he'd be able to find that right moment in there someplace.

The two of them weren't three steps into the room when Vincent grabbed the microphone for an announcement. "Hey, people, listen up! I want everyone to know that my good buddy Tanner has just chauffeured the love of my life to the party. Let it be known that Katie and I have set the date. We marry tomorrow, and everyone here is invited to the reception."

Tanner rolled his eyes as the room exploded in laughter. "In your dreams!" he yelled back. "Katie and I just eloped—that's why we're late."

Tanner slipped an arm through Katherine's and led her over to the food table, where Cory was refilling his plate for what Tanner guessed was at least the third time. Cory was one of those guys who could pack away more calories than most could even count. At 5'5", he was nearly as round as he was tall. But with Cory, no one ever seemed to notice since his winning personality kept everyone around him in stitches. Cory's fondest aspiration in life was to become a great actor, like Harrison Ford or Tom Cruise. Tanner never doubted that Cory could reach his goal, with the possible exception that he'd become more of a Danny DeVito.

Tanner and Katherine nearly had their plates filled when Brandon joined them. To Tanner's pleasant surprise, Brandon was more interested in showing off a graduation present from his grandfather than he was in Katherine. "Take a look at this," Brandon exclaimed, holding out what appeared to be a very old pocket watch. "Granddad promised me this years ago, but I wasn't supposed to get it until I got married."

"Your granddad is a smart man," Cory cut in. "By the time you hooked some poor female, he'd be too old and blind to see you get this watch."

Brandon ignored Cory. "Look at it!" he said again. "Have you ever seen anything like it?"

Tanner took the watch and held it where both he and Katherine could examine it. It was pure gold and had an elaborate engraving of a telescope against the backdrop of a star-filled sky on the face. "Your granddad was an astronomer, wasn't he?" Tanner asked, realizing the significance of the engraving.

"Yeah," Brandon responded, smiling ear to ear. "He wanted me to follow suit, and he was influential in my choosing to study another branch of science."

"Computer science," Tanner laughed. "A far cry from the stars, unless they happen to be part of your screen saver."

"It's still science," Brandon argued. "Important science by today's standards."

"What's the value of the watch?" Katherine asked.

"Don't know and don't care," Brandon said, retrieving the watch and opening it for all to see. "Granddad put this inscription in it just for me," he pointed out.

Tanner leaned in to read the inscription. *Reach for the stars, and even on the darkest night, I'll always be there with you.* "Wow, that is something," he remarked.

Cory spoke up again. "Maybe I should hold the watch for you. We all know how forgetful you computer nerds can be. I wouldn't want you to lose it, man."

"You're lucky I even let you look at this," Brandon laughed. "I'd never let the watch into hands that might get mustard all over it."

Just then, Tanner noticed Vincent walking toward them. To his surprise, Brandon gently shoved him and Katherine toward the dance floor. "Go have some fun, you two," he said. "I'll run interference as long as I can, but don't count on it being too long. Not from the look in those beady eyes."

Tanner hesitated only long enough to drop off his and Katherine's plates at an empty table, then quickly ushered her to the already-crowded dance floor. A glance backward revealed Vincent politely nodding while listening to Brandon talk about his watch. For an instant, Tanner's eyes met Vincent's, and he knew the competition for Katie wasn't over. He figured he'd be seeing more of Vincent real soon, but what he hadn't counted on was not seeing Brandon again—ever.

* * *

An approaching vehicle caught Tanner's attention. Thinking it might be his bus, he strained for a glimpse through the fog. To his surprise, it wasn't the bus at all. It was the very same taxi he'd been riding in when it broke down only minutes earlier. Jumping up, he waved at the driver, who ignored him and passed on by. "Wouldn't you know it," Tanner grumbled disgustedly as he noticed another rider in the backseat. "That guy has the heart of a crocodile."

Tanner returned to the bench and sat down to wait, completely unaware of two invisible angels who watched him with deep interest.

CHAPTER 2

Mitzi Palmer was a highly dedicated guardian angel, and had been ever since being assigned to the position half a decade ago. Her commitment to the job had never been questioned, nor had her ability to perform the duties of a guardian angel—not until now, at least. This strange new event did leave her feeling a bit edgy over the possibility that the authorities might be losing their confidence in her. Why else would they send reinforcements to assist in her calling? True, this Brandon Cheney seemed nice enough, and he certainly wasn't the pushy type. Maybe she was reading more into the situation than she should. "Would you mind explaining it one more time?" she asked, doing her best to maintain her patience. "Why exactly have you been assigned as my backup?"

Brandon shifted his weight nervously from one leg to the other, indicating he was just as uncomfortable with this new arrangement as Mitzi was. "I'm not really your backup," he attempted to explain. "You're Tanner's permanently assigned guardian angel; I'm only a special-assignment angel. I'll be with you just long enough to pull a few loose ends together, then he'll be all yours again."

The term *special-assignment angel* was one Mitzi hadn't heard until Brandon showed up an hour earlier referring to himself as one. She could kick herself for being so dense. After all, she had been in the world of angels more than half a decade now. One would think that by this time she might be a little more familiar with the way things worked over here. Then again, she reasoned, with Tanner Nelson being her first and only angelic assignment, she hadn't had much opportunity for exploring other celestial avenues. "I hope you realize

I'm not familiar with special-assignment angels," she admitted. "I still have a lot to learn over here."

"*You* have a lot to learn?" Brandon laughed. "Hey, don't think I'm a celestial rocket scientist. In fact, I was sort of hoping you might fill me in on a few things."

Mitzi's brow raised quizzically. Brandon wanted information from her? Now there was a twist. No one had ever asked her angelic opinion before. "Fill you in on what, exactly?" she cautiously asked. "The only thing I know about is guardian angels, and even then I know about enough to fill half a thimble."

Brandon shrugged. "We make a pair, don't we? So, tell me what you know about guardian angels."

"Well, let's see . . . as a guardian angel, it's my responsibility to monitor the welfare of my assigned mortal." She glanced at Tanner, still sitting on the bench at the bus stop. "Him," she said with a nod in Tanner's direction.

Brandon's eyes shifted to Tanner, then back to Mitzi. "How did they go about picking you to be Tanner's guardian?" he asked.

Mitzi retreated to her own thoughts for a moment before attempting to answer this question. It was something she hadn't considered all that much. "I assume I was picked because my personality meshes with Tanner Nelson's," she said at last. "My supervising angel is constantly going on about how well suited our personalities are for each other."

Brandon rubbed the back of his neck. "You think angels are picked for certain positions because someone assumes their personality suits the task? Doesn't that seem like shallow criteria to you?"

Mitzi did a double take. "What do mean?" she asked.

"I mean a person's qualifications for a job should go a lot deeper than just his or her personality. I'd think an applicant would be scrutinized by one of those celestial computers everyone but me seems to have on a desk in their very own office."

"Computers?" Mitzi asked, shocked. "That's the craziest thing I ever heard. Computers shouldn't be used to evaluate people—people should evaluate people. Computers are fine for keeping records and that sort of thing, but evaluating whether or not I'm suited for an assignment? I think not."

Brandon obviously wasn't buying it. "Don't underestimate computers, Mitzi. They can do some pretty fantastic stuff. Especially the computers they use over here."

"Well, personally, I'm glad it was a living being who appointed me to my assignment. And I'm glad I was matched up with Tanner. He's lots of fun."

Brandon couldn't help but smile. "You think Tanner's fun, do you? What is it you like, the intrigue of him being a cop?"

"He's not a cop," Mitzi corrected. "He's an investigator, and a really good one."

"Cop, investigator, what's the difference? It all adds up to intrigue, and I suspect that's what you like about working with him."

"Maybe so," she admitted. "Is it a crime to enjoy a good measure of intrigue?"

Brandon's smile widened. "No, it's not a crime. And knowing Tanner the way I do, I can see how being his guardian angel could be fun. Maybe *exciting* is a better word. Never boring, that's for sure. Which brings me to my next question. I've observed some guardian angels who look after more than one mortal. Why is it you're assigned to Tanner and no one else?"

"Because I'm still just a bud on the angelic vine," she laughingly explained. "All guardian angels start with a single client. I'll be given added assignments when I'm ready for them."

"That makes sense, I guess."

"My clientele will probably grow when Tanner takes a wife and starts a family. It's quite common for one guardian angel to look after an entire family."

"Don't hold your breath waiting for this one to get married," Brandon joked. "Tanner has an aversion to commitment, and has ever since I've known him."

"I know that, but I'm sure when the right one comes along, he'll loosen up."

"How long you been working with Tanner now?"

"About five years. Why?"

"Only five years? How much do you know about his life before that time?"

"Not much, I suppose."

"Well, as far as Tanner's concerned, the right one slipped through his fingers about three years before you came into the picture. Her name was Katherine Dalton."

"Lovely name. But you're right, I didn't know about her. I suppose I should take time to research Tanner's early life; I just never have."

"So, how much time do you have to spend with Tanner? Are you on his shoulder twenty-four-seven?"

Mitzi laughed. "No way! I'm not married to my assignment. I have a celestial life of my own to lead. I drop in on him once or twice a day. You know, just to see how things are going." She paused to look at Brandon. "You do understand how the Celestial Monitoring Department works, don't you?"

"Yeah, sort of. I've heard of it, at least. I've never visited their facility or anything. Have you?"

"Once. I got the grand tour during the orientation for my guardian angel position. It's an elaborate facility, let me tell you. It's almost scary knowing how every mortal alive is under their constant observation."

"That's what I'm told," Brandon said. "I admit, it is a little scary. It's probably better we didn't know about it when we were under their microscope, wouldn't you say?"

"Definitely better. But they sure make my job easier. If Tanner gets in the slightest trouble, I'm instantly notified." Mitzi paused a moment, then asked a question of her own. "How long has it been since you departed the mortal world for our realm of angels?"

"I've been here about eight years now."

"And have you been a special-assignment angel all that time?"

"Oh, no, I'm regularly attached to the Celestial Records Department. This special-assignment thing is a first. Some things about it are going to take some getting used to."

"Like what?" she asked.

"Like the way I was allowed to cause the engine to stall in that cab. I was never permitted to do such a thing in my job at the records department."

Mitzi had been a little surprised at that, too. As a guardian angel, she wasn't allowed to interfere in any way with Tanner's life other than to make suggestions to his subconscious mind as she deemed appropriate. Brandon had explained that he was permitted to disable the taxi because the authorities wanted Tanner to miss his scheduled flight. For reasons Brandon apparently understood but hadn't shared with Mitzi yet, the authorities wanted Tanner's arrival back at Phoenix to be postponed a few hours. After Brandon disabled the taxi, he went on to assure Mitzi he wasn't permitted to do things like that on an ongoing basis, but only as he was given specific permission. "What exactly did you do to the taxi?" she asked. "I notice it started again after Tanner was out of the picture."

"I caused a temporary clog in the fuel line," Brandon explained. "No use in preventing the cabbie from doing a full day's work just because Tanner needed to be delayed."

By now, Mitzi was feeling better about Brandon's one-time assignment, more confident it wasn't so much a reflection on her ability as it was something the authorities felt Brandon was more qualified for since he and Tanner had been such good friends. She was still certain Brandon would need her help in accomplishing the assignment, whatever it was. No one knew Tanner better than Mitzi, and no one could reach his subconscious mind the way she could. The ease she always had in reaching Tanner with her suggestions was one thing that made working with him so enjoyable. Some other guardian angels Mitzi knew weren't so lucky with their mortal clients. Oftentimes a mortal just wouldn't listen to the promptings of an angel. They were the ones who invariably ended up in trouble.

Mitzi couldn't deny how secretly good it made her feel when Brandon ran into problems getting Tanner to reminisce about the graduation party. No matter how hard Brandon tried, he just couldn't get through. That's when she stepped in. One simple suggestion from her lips, and Tanner was reliving the event in detail. She was, however, a little perturbed that Brandon didn't credit her for the help. He just shrugged it off without a word.

Mitzi weighed her next question carefully, finally concluding she had the right to know. "Why did the authorities want Tanner to miss his flight?" she asked. "You mentioned wanting him back in Phoenix later than planned, but why?"

"It's all part of my special assignment, Mitzi. There's an appointment the authorities want Tanner to keep at Phoenix Sky Harbor

Airport, and that appointment requires him to be at the airport at an exact time."

Mitzi couldn't help but feel as though Brandon was putting her off by using the term *appointment* without explaining what the appointment was about, but she let it go for the time being and approached the subject from a fresh angle. "The graduation party you wanted Tanner to remember? Does that have something to do with your assignment?"

Brandon grew solemn. "It has everything to do with it," he responded. "If you like, I can run a hologram replay of the party so you can see for yourself what happened there."

"You can do that?" Mitzi asked excitedly.

"Yeah, I work with holograms all the time in the records department. When it comes to researching history, there's really no other way. Running a hologram of the party would be a snap."

"How exciting!" Mitzi exclaimed. "I've only seen two celestial holograms, and what an experience they were. I'd love to have you show me one of the party—if you're sure it's all right."

"I don't know why it wouldn't be." Brandon shrugged. "I have the skill, and no one told me I couldn't use it in this assignment." He snapped his fingers, and Mitzi caught her breath in excitement as a real hologram opened up right before her eyes. She was amazed at how these things worked. It was like she really became a part of the scene being depicted, even feeling what the participants were feeling at the time the event actually occurred. She could see how invaluable these would be as tools for researching historical events. She quickly recognized two faces in the crowd, one a slightly younger version of Tanner, and the other . . . "Oh, my!" she gasped. "You were at that party, Brandon."

"I was there. Let me give you a little history to set the stage. Five of my friends and I had just come from the graduation exercises at U of A in Flagstaff. Tanner, you already know. The others are Cory Harper, Vincent Wagner, and Troy Adams." Brandon pointed to each as he said their names.

"That's only four," Mitzi observed. "You mentioned a fifth."

"The fifth is the beautiful woman standing next to Tanner," Brandon replied. "Remember me mentioning Katherine Dalton?"

Mitzi's attention instantly zeroed in on Katherine. She just had to know what the woman who could so completely captivate Tanner's attention looked like. "She is beautiful, isn't she," Mitzi said.

"She's a lot more than beautiful," Brandon said. "Katherine has that special something that reaches out and grabs a man's heart. In the years I knew her, she had more guys chasing her than I could even count."

Mitzi looked closer at Katherine, trying to understand just what this special something was. Regardless, she could tell by looking at Tanner that this woman had reached out and grabbed his heart. "He is in love with her, isn't he?" Mitzi remarked. "Tanner, I mean."

Brandon laughed. "Tanner wasn't the only one of us in love with Katherine. Cory, Vincent, Troy, and even yours truly fell for her at one time or another. Looking back on it now, I can see that the only two who were seriously in love with her were Tanner and Vincent. For the rest of us, it was more or less an infatuation. We didn't know it then, though."

Mitzi was still trying to analyze this when a voice over the loud-speaker system at the party caught her attention. She looked to see the person Brandon had identified as Vincent Wagner standing by a microphone. *Hey, people, listen up! I want everyone to know that my good buddy Tanner has just chauffeured the love of my life to the party. Let it be known that Katie and I have set the date. We marry tomorrow, and everyone here is invited to the reception.*

"Katherine and Vincent were going to be married?" Mitzi asked in surprise.

"Not really," Brandon laughed. "It was a game between the five of us. We all left our standing proposal at Katherine's feet. Vincent would have given half his father's fortune for that announcement to be true, but it wasn't."

"Vincent's father was rather wealthy?" Mitzi questioned.

"Rich as they come."

In your dreams! Tanner suddenly yelled back at Vincent. *Katie and I just eloped—that's why we're late.*

By this time, Mitzi got the picture. She watched as Tanner led Katherine over to the food table, where they joined Brandon. "What's that you're showing the others?" she asked.

"It's a pocket watch my granddad had given me for a graduation present."

"It looks like a lovely one."

"Yeah, it was. I didn't get much time to enjoy it though. I want you to notice what a nice guy I was here. If you look, you'll see Vincent walking over to join the group. I knew his intention was to take Katherine away from Tanner, so I played the martyr and urged Tanner to get her out on the dance floor before Vincent got there."

"Oh, I see. If you couldn't have Katherine's affections for yourself, at least you could choose which of the others got her affection? From the look on Vincent's face, I'd say he wasn't too pleased with you right about then."

"That would be an accurate appraisal. This is where Vincent spills punch on my good shirt, and I think if you watch closely you'll see it was no accident."

Mitzi could hardly help laughing at what she saw. Brandon was right. Vincent walked up and deliberately tripped, spilling punch all over Brandon. Then he whispered something in Brandon's ear. "What's he saying?" Mitzi asked.

"Something about me wishing I were dead if I ever came between him and Katherine again. You know, just a friendly little comment about me getting the best of him this time around. What you're seeing now are some of my last moments in mortality. In less than ten hours, I'll be crossing the line."

"What happened, Brandon?"

"It all started with the punch on my shirt. I wasn't ready to leave the party, and I couldn't stay there without cleaning up. There's only one downstairs bathroom in the cabin, and it was occupied, but Vincent had given everyone specific orders not to go upstairs for any reason. These were orders he was passing on from his father, who owned the place and had an office on the top floor. But the way I saw it, it was Vincent's fault I needed a place to clean up."

"You went upstairs looking for another bathroom?" Mitzi guessed.

"After I made darn sure no one was looking."

Mitzi watched as the hologram of Brandon climbed the stairs and stepped out of sight down a long hall. One at a time, he checked the doors. "I should have given up when I found them all locked," Brandon explained. "But no, I had to keep trying. Watch what happens at this next door."

As Mitzi looked on, she saw Brandon try the door only to find it locked the same as the others. But when he tugged a little, he discovered the latch hadn't completely snapped. It slipped, and the door pulled open. "Of all the rooms to find my way inside of, it had to be that one." Brandon sounded disbelieving. "It turned out to be Zachary Wagner's personal office. All it took was one look at his computer, and I was hooked. Computers have advanced a long way in the mortal world since that day, but at that time, his was state of the art. I couldn't resist getting a look at it. There was no bathroom in the office, but there was a wet bar I used to mop up my shirt. Then I headed straight to the computer."

Mitzi watched the Brandon in the hologram sit down at the computer and switch it on. At that point, the angel Brandon suddenly brought an end to the hologram. "Why did you do that?" Mitzi pressed. "I wanted to see the rest of it."

"There's nothing more to see, really. Just me fooling around with the computer. I'll cut to the chase and tell you what happened next."

Mitzi would rather have watched it in a hologram, but she listened to his story instead. "I found that the files were password protected, but it was just too much of a challenge for me to pass up. I broke the password in less than five minutes. I should have been satisfied with that, but my shirt was still wet, so I figured I could kill some time while it dried. No one knew what I was up to, or so I supposed at the time. So, what could it hurt?"

"Are you saying someone did know?"

"Zachary had the room wired right down to a video camera that positively identified me. I should have caught it, but I was so darn interested in that computer I tuned everything else out. As I searched through the files, I soon realized what I had stumbled onto. It seems our boy hadn't acquired his wealth selling Girl Scout cookies. I had unwittingly uncovered proof that Wagner Aerospace was selling reclaimed components to NASA under the guise that the parts were brand-new."

"This was definitely something you couldn't ignore, right?"

"No way could I ignore it! At that time, NASA had already lost one shuttle because of maintenance problems. I couldn't just sit by and let those faulty components find their way onboard another craft. I had to do something, and I had to have the proof in hand. I searched through drawers until I found a blank computer disk, and then I burned a copy of the incriminating file. I wasn't sure where to go from there, but I knew someone who would be."

"Tanner?" Mitzi guessed.

"Yeah. Even back then, Tanner was heavy into law-enforcement stuff. I knew he'd know exactly what to do. I shut down the computer and slipped out of the office, then made my way downstairs to join the others. To my disappointment, I learned that Tanner and Katherine had already left. Katherine hadn't told any of us why she wanted to get home to Mesa as soon as possible, only that she did. She made a deal with Tanner to drive her there, and they took off while I was playing games with Zachary's computer. I slipped back into Wagner's office, where I used his phone to call Tanner's apartment. Since Tanner was driving Katherine down the mountain to Mesa, I knew it would be the wee hours of the morning before he got home. All I could do was leave a message for him to call as soon as he got in. How was I to know I wouldn't be there to take the call?"

As Mitzi was contemplating all this, she glanced up to see a bus rounding the corner in London. "Would you look at this?" she said. "I do believe Tanner's transportation has arrived."

"You're right," Brandon agreed. "And just late enough to ensure Tanner misses his flight. So far, so good. The plan is right on course." Brandon wet his lips. "If you'd like a bit of a vacation from Tanner, I think I can take it alone from here. Until my assignment is closed out, I mean. After that, he's all yours again."

Mitzi straightened to her full frame. "Are you trying to get rid of me?" she pressed.

"No, no, nothing like that. I honestly thought you might like a break."

"Well, I wouldn't, thank you. I can be a lot of help with your assignment if you'll let me."

"I'm sure. I was impressed with the way you got Tanner thinking about the graduation party after he turned me off cold. I'd love having your help."

Well, what do you know? He did notice. "Okay." She grinned. "Where do we go from here?"

"A good question, Mitzi. From here, we pay a visit to the reason Tanner had to miss his regular flight. You saw her in the hologram, now you get to meet her up close."

"Katherine Dalton?" Mitzi guessed.

"Yep. Katherine Dalton. Come on, let's go."

CHAPTER 3

Katherine glanced out the little round window to see they were flying over billows of cotton-candy clouds—clouds so thick it almost seemed she could step out and walk on them. A melancholy ache tugged at her heart as faces of friends and loved ones she was leaving behind flashed before her eyes. When would she ever see them again? The bitter reality was she didn't know. A lot of miles stretched between Melbourne, Australia, and Phoenix, Arizona. These past eight years in Melbourne had been amazing, but to Katherine, home would always be the Arizona desert. And in her heart, she knew it was time to go home.

Luck had been with her as she managed a window seat in an empty row. Thankfully, she wouldn't be pressed into polite conversation with some stranger. That was good. This was one of those times when all she wanted was to be left alone. She lowered her seat and closed her eyes with the intention of catching a nap.

* * *

"So this is Katherine Dalton?" Mitzi remarked, staring down at Katherine's relaxed face. "I think she's even more beautiful now than in the hologram eight years ago."

"She's the most beautiful woman I've ever laid eyes on," Brandon said.

"So, how does she fit into your assignment?"

"How do I put this?" Brandon began. "You know that aversion to commitment I mentioned Tanner having? Let's just say I have to find a way to get him past it. The authorities feel second chances are in order since these two blew their first one."

Mitzi's eyes shifted to Brandon, then back to Katherine. "The authorities sent you to play Cupid?"

Brandon appeared uncomfortable at the way Mitzi had put it. "It's only part of my assignment," he said. "I have other things to do too."

"But you're supposed to get Brandon and Katherine together, is that what you're saying?"

"Well, you know, since I can't have her myself, I suppose it's only right she be given a shot at second best. Yeah, I'm supposed to get them together."

Mitzi was liking the sound of this assignment better by the minute. In her mind, Tanner was missing out on so much because he didn't have a special someone in his life. Here was her chance to rectify the problem. She wasn't sure what else this special assignment of Brandon's might entail, but this part was right up her alley. "Okay," she said. "If we want to get the two of them together, don't you think this might be a good time to plant a suggestion in her mind to get her thinking about him?"

"That's exactly what I plan to do, Mitzi. Those were my precise instructions."

Mitzi smiled. "Well, Mr. Cheney, in that case I'd say you're in need of my expertise. You may be good with holograms, but I'm the expert at planting suggestions. Why don't you just stand out of the way and let me handle this part of our special assignment."

"*Our* assignment?" Brandon asked with a laugh.

"Yes, *our* assignment." Her response came with a distinct air of confidence. "Admit it, Brandon, you need me. I can have the lady thinking about the gentleman long before you could even draw her out of the sleep she's about to drift into."

Brandon rubbed his chin as he retreated into thought. "Why not?" he said with a smile. "Be my guest, Mitzi. Do your thing."

* * *

Try as she might, Katherine couldn't clear her mind enough to allow sleep to settle in. It was like a little voice from somewhere deep in her subconscious kept whispering the name *Tanner Nelson*. The fact that his name surfaced wasn't surprising since she was on her way home to Arizona, where she and Tanner had built so many memories as college students. Who knew what might have happened between them if she had only handled things differently back then? Why she wanted to wait until the last second to tell him she was leaving for Melbourne, Australia, was a question she still couldn't answer with any real rationale. She had known about the pending move weeks in advance, but she just couldn't bring herself to spring it on him. It was the coward's way out, she knew that now, and it was a mistake she also knew she could end up paying for for the rest of her life. But how was she to know Tanner would react the way he did? She was almost certain he had intended to propose that night, but she might be wrong. Somehow it was hard to picture Tanner as being the marrying kind, at least back then. Had he just taken the news of her move as an excuse to let her walk out of his life? She just didn't know. But still, she should have treated him more honestly. He did deserve that much.

Thinking about him now, she couldn't help wondering if he still lived in Phoenix. Then a staggering thought crossed her mind. What if they should ever run into each other? What would she say to him? What could she say?

Then her thoughts shifted to her decision to leave Arizona—and Tanner—eight years ago. It wasn't like she *had* to go to Australia. She could have stayed behind and let her parents go without her. After all, they were capable adults who could have gotten along perfectly well on their own. But that was a possibility Katherine would never have considered. With her father changing careers so late in life, and with that career change taking him halfway around the world, she refused to believe either he or her mother wouldn't need her—at least until they had time to put down some roots. She never anticipated staying away from home as long as she had. Things had just worked out that way.

Wherever Tanner was now, and whatever his circumstances, Katherine was positive he'd be carrying a badge and gun. Law enforcement was his passion back then, and she knew him well enough to know it would be now. Again she tried unsuccessfully to put thoughts of him aside. Her memories shifted to the drive home from Flagstaff following the graduation party. Tanner had been in such a great mood that night. Katherine remembered how she wanted to savor every minute with him before the time came for her inevitable confession.

Tanner had suggested a late-night snack at a Denny's restaurant on the way home. It sounded like fun, and it actually turned into an early breakfast after checking the menu. Katherine could almost smell the hotcakes and eggs. But the part she remembered most was their conversation. Was that really eight years ago? Incredible. Absolutely incredible.

* * *

"So, how does it feel, pretty lady?" Tanner asked as he buttered a slice of toast. "Being a certified teacher, I mean. It's always been your dream, and *voilà*—here you are."

Katherine's smile didn't reach her eyes. Her time with Tanner was growing short, and the prospect of the confession she'd soon have to make wasn't getting any more appealing. "It feels nice," she responded.

"That's it?" he chuckled. "Nice? I sort of expected you'd be a bit more enthused."

"I'm sorry, Tanner. I know this is a big day for you in the dream department, with the law-enforcement career practically in your pocket and all. It's just that, well . . ."

Tanner bit off the corner of his toast and stared as her voice trailed off. "It's just that what?" he prompted.

"Nothing," she said. "I'm in a silly mood, that's all."

Tanner dropped the toast and stared even harder. "I'm not buying it, Katie," he said. "Something's wrong, and I want to know what it is."

I can't do this . . . Katherine told herself. *I have to tell him, but how?* Tanner's eyes were burning through her, and he refused to look away. She held off until she could stand it no longer. "All right!" she blurted out. "There is something bothering me."

Tanner moved his plate to one side and leaned a little closer. "And that is?" he calmly asked.

Katherine brushed her hair off one shoulder. "I, uh, applied for a job as a history teacher. I've been accepted. I start two weeks from Monday."

"That's a bad thing?" Tanner asked, not lowering his eyes one inch.

"No . . . ! That is, yes . . . !" She drew a breath. "My job is at the University of Melbourne."

Tanner's eyes widened, and he slowly straightened. "Melbourne, Australia?" he guessed.

"Yes," she gulped, unable to contain one hot tear that trickled slowly down her cheek.

He was still looking at her, but his eyes reflected a mood change she so desperately wanted to reverse. "Going to Melbourne, Australia, eh?"

She only nodded.

Tanner feigned a shallow smile. "That sounds pretty awesome. Maybe you'll get to meet that Dundee fellow. Or should I call him a bloke?"

Removing a tissue from her purse, Katherine tried to smile as she dabbed both eyes. "My dad bought a ranch there. He's always wanted to live in Australia, and he's always wanted to try his hand at ranching."

"Ranching, you say? Sounds like something your dad might do."

"He waited until I was near graduation before springing this on me. Mom pressured him into telling me a few weeks back."

"Weeks? You've known that long?"

"I probably should have told you. I didn't tell anyone. You're the first to know, if that's any consolation."

"Hey, you wanted to keep it to yourself. I'm sure you had your reasons."

She had her reasons all right. They all involved her being a coward. Katherine knew she had fallen in love with Tanner, and she thought he had fallen in love with her. She was afraid of losing what they had and didn't want to chance it one second sooner than necessary. "The only reason I didn't tell you is because I hate good-byes," she lied. "I wanted to hold off as long as possible."

Tanner wiped his mouth and dropped the napkin to his lap. "You say you start teaching in two weeks? That means you'll be leaving soon. Will there be time for a party at least?"

Her eyes lowered. "No, I fly out tomorrow afternoon."

"Tomorrow?!" The sound of his voice exploded in her ears. "You're leaving tomorrow and you're just now telling me?"

Katherine knew Tanner might be hurt when he learned of her plans, but she had no idea it would hit him as hard as it did. It couldn't be all that bad, could it? They could write, and they could talk to each other over the phone. She wouldn't be gone forever, and they could pick up where they left off when she returned. As she fought to keep the sobs from showing, she noticed Tanner pull something from his pocket. It was a small black box, which he fumbled with for several seconds. Katherine couldn't be positive, but she was almost certain it was a ring box. Was he about to propose? Her heart sank as Tanner returned the unopened box to his pocket. "What was that?" Katherine asked. The question slipped out before she could think.

"Nothing really," Tanner answered, the sparkle that had been in his voice all night now missing. "I was going to play a joke, that's all. Somehow it doesn't seem very appropriate now. Anyway, it wouldn't have been all that funny without the guys here to see it."

"That was no joke. You were about to propose!" Again, the words just seemed to tumble out.

"No, no! It was just a joke!"

* * *

Katherine was remembering her hurt upon hearing those words when the flight attendant's voice brought her around. "Would you like a pillow?" the woman asked, smiling warmly.

"Yes, thank you," Katherine replied. "That would be nice."

As the flight attendant walked away, Katherine punched the pillow and placed it behind her head. She closed her eyes, hoping thoughts of Tanner would leave now. No such luck. This time her mind's eye shifted to the scene just after the breakfast at Denny's. It was their final good-bye on the front porch of her parents' old home in Mesa. Katherine knew she would never forget the look in Tanner's eyes. Was it hurt or betrayal? She was never quite sure. But his face revealed a deep enough emotion that she realized it was the end to what might have been a wonderful dream. He didn't even kiss her; he simply touched her cheek, then turned and walked away.

Katherine had written to Tanner from Australia, just as she promised. Three times, in fact, but no answer came. Did she have regrets? How could she not? But if she had it to do all over again, what would she do differently? That was another lifetime ago. She and Tanner were so young. Young enough that all she could see was the light of the present day and not the greater light of so many tomorrows on the horizon.

A great many of those tomorrows had come and gone since the emptiness of that night. Sadly, the emptiness was never filled. Katherine drew a deep breath, closed her eyes, and at last fell into a restless sleep.

CHAPTER 4

Flying had always been a passion for Tanner, but flying as a passenger on an airliner was his least favorite way of doing it. He much preferred being in the pilot seat, but it was a bit difficult justifying use of the company jet for an assignment on the opposite side of the Atlantic Ocean. Thanks to his personal digital assistant, he was able to use this time to pound out a stack of reports that otherwise he'd have to face back in the home office. Reports were the one part of Tanner's job he had never liked. Why couldn't life be more like the movies, where James Bond spent all his time solving crimes and zero time doing reports?

The flight had been pleasant enough, in spite of the fact that it was four hours behind his intended schedule. It was a welcome sound when the captain's voice finally came over the intercom announcing their arrival at Phoenix Sky Harbor Airport. "Good afternoon, ladies and gentlemen, this is your captain. We'll be dropping down for our final approach in the next few minutes. We'd like to ask you to take your seat and remain buckled in for the rest of the flight. We anticipate a smooth landing and should be docking at our assigned gate in approximately fifteen minutes. It's a clear day in Phoenix with an airport temperature reported to be ninety-six degrees—a little warmer than what you left in London, but not as warm as might be expected from a June day in Phoenix."

Tanner raised his seat and snapped his safety belt in place. The pilot's prediction of a smooth landing turned out to be accurate, and with Tanner traveling first class, he was near enough to the exit to be one of the first off the plane. His only carry-on was his laptop, and he never bothered with check-in luggage. With the number of air miles he logged, it was easier to have his luggage sent directly to his apartment. If he wasn't home when it arrived, the apartment manager would hold it for him, a much easier arrangement than standing in line waiting for it—something Tanner didn't do well.

Leaving the gate, Tanner made his way through the crowd toward the elevator, where he intended to ride up to the parking level. As usual, he had told no one when to expect him home. That way, he could make an uninterrupted beeline for his apartment, soak an hour or so in the jacuzzi, then sleep a few hours to help shake the jet lag. This was a small luxury Tanner allowed himself. He'd simply check in at the office in the morning and, as usual, no one would be the wiser.

* * *

Being angels, Mitzi and Brandon had little trouble keeping track of Tanner even when he was engulfed by the crowd. Mitzi tingled with excitement at the anticipation of where this special assignment was headed—not that being Tanner Nelson's guardian angel wasn't exciting enough on a day-to-day basis. But this assignment held the promise of something greatly lacking in Tanner's life—a promise of romance. Mitzi was certain the assignment would run much deeper than just getting Tanner and Katherine back together, but that's the part that interested her—for the moment at least.

"There's Katherine directly ahead!" Brandon suddenly exclaimed. "She's disembarking at gate ten, Mitzi."

Mitzi glanced up. "Do you think we'll have to intervene to get the two of them together?"

"I don't think so," Brandon explained. "When it comes to something like precision timing, I figure the authorities will take charge personally. It looks to me like the two of them are already on a collision course."

"I think you're right," Mitzi cheerfully agreed. "Isn't this exciting?"

"Yeah," Brandon grumbled. "What could be more exciting than watching my best friend and the only woman I ever thought I was in love with get together?"

Mitzi found this amusing, but kept it to herself.

* * *

Tanner thought nothing of it when the woman stepped directly into his path—not until he chanced to glance at her face. There was a split second before recognition set in, and another split second of denial before the full impact of who it was struck home. "Katie?!" he gasped while staring into a set of eyes just as startled as his own.

"Tanner?" came her stammering reply.

For the next few moments, the two of them remained silent. "Why are you in Phoenix?" Tanner numbly heard himself ask. Katherine's lips moved, but no sound emerged.

Tanner discovered himself captivated by her beauty, a beauty that had only intensified in the years since last seeing her. Her hair was shorter now, and there was look of maturity about her. "Why are you here?" he asked again, shock gripping him.

"I—I've come home . . ." she somehow managed to respond.

Tanner rubbed his face briskly, almost expecting her to disappear. He blinked three times, and she was still there, alive and vibrant as ever. Tanner felt someone bump into him. "Pardon me, sir!" came a sharp voice. "Do you mind?" Tanner instantly realized that a man behind him was wanting to use the pay phone. Taking Katherine's bags from her, he quickly led the way to a more secluded spot. "What do you mean you've come home?" he asked. "For a visit, or what?"

"No, not for a visit. I'm here to stay. I've accepted a teaching position at ASU West." The inflection in Katherine's voice was a dead giveaway that she was just as nervous about this chance meeting as was Tanner. "The job doesn't start until September, but I wanted some time to get things in order," she went on to explain.

Tanner's heart was pounding. Could this be real, or was he dreaming? It wouldn't be his first dream of Katherine Dalton to reach a disappointing end at the sound of an alarm clock. He nodded, still amazed that she was standing in front of him. "You've really come home to stay?" he asked.

"Yes."

"Your job at Melbourne didn't work out?"

"It worked out fine. I fell in love with the Australian people."

"Your parents? Did things work out well for them?"

"They couldn't be happier. Dad's like a kid with a new toy. He took to ranching like a bee to a honeysuckle. He and Mom have tons of friends there now, mostly from church. They've reached a point where I felt like I could come home without disrupting their world." She paused a moment, smiled, and then added, "So, here I am."

"Yes," Tanner responded with a smile of his own. "So you are."

A long, awkward moment passed before either of them spoke. It was Katherine who jumped in first. "I suppose I'd better pick up the rest of my luggage. I brought along two more suitcases. I'm having everything else shipped over."

Tanner felt a churning in his stomach. He had to do something—he couldn't just let her walk away. "Will you be staying at your folks' old house?" he asked, then realized what a dumb question it was since he knew her folks had sold their house years ago.

"Oh, no," she said with a shaky laugh. "That place is gone. I'll just get a room for the first few days until I can find a suitable apartment."

He cautiously asked his next question. "So, is your husband along?" He instantly wished he could take it back or find a way to hide under the edge of the carpet.

"I—I'm not married," she responded.

"Oh, good. I mean—oh man . . ." Tanner's face burned with embarrassment. "I meant to say it's good that you've come home, not that you're not married."

"Oh . . ." She nervously wet her lips. "How about you, Tanner? Are you—married yet?"

"Uh, no. Not me."

This time her smile seemed more real. "I didn't think you would be. It sort of looks like neither of us is the marrying kind."

"Yeah, looks like."

She drew in a deep breath and let it out very slowly. "I suppose I really should get down to baggage claim. Wouldn't want to lose my suitcases at a time like this."

"No, I guess not. That could be bad." Tanner handed back the items he had helped her with.

"It was really nice seeing you again," she said.

"Yeah, for me, too."

* * *

Katherine's heart was pounding as she contemplated stepping onto the escalator and letting it sweep her away from this chance meeting. What a strange coincidence it was. She had wondered what might happen if she ever ran into Tanner again, and she'd barely made it off the plane before it had happened. She'd tried not to stare, but she couldn't help it. Tanner had aged some, but it only enhanced his already-rugged handsomeness. He still sported a full head of jet-black hair, and his dark eyes still held that fascinating hint of mystery. His face contained a stubble of beard, which she assumed was there only because he hadn't had the chance to shave yet. Not that it mattered to her. Why should it matter? This was just a chance meeting, nothing more. He'd be going his way, and she'd be going hers.

She couldn't help but notice the little dimple in the center of his chin, the dimple she had always loved. And he still radiated his trademark air of confidence. It was so easy to see why she had once fallen in love with the guy.

"Well," she said, "have yourself a wonderful day. Maybe we'll run into each other again sometime?"

"Maybe."

She couldn't stop the tears from welling up as she walked toward the escalator, but she kept her head turned so he couldn't see. Why did it suddenly feel like the walls were closing in on her? Tanner was just a guy she once knew, nothing more . . . so why did she want him to stop her now? All of a sudden, she wondered why she had thought coming home was such a good idea, and she wanted to be someplace where she could cry without shame.

"Wait, Katie!" Tanner called out.

She froze in her tracks, and ever so gradually turned to face him. She hoped he wouldn't notice she had been crying.

"I was wondering," he began. "Could we, you know, maybe get together sometime for a bite to eat?"

Had he asked what she thought he had? "I'd like that," she said, unable to keep her voice from cracking.

"Do you have a cell phone?"

"Yes!" She dropped her suitcase and began fumbling through her purse for something to write on.

"Don't worry about that," Tanner said, hurrying over to where she stood. "Here, put your number in this." He handed her his PDA. She punched in her number and gave it back. He looked at it and grinned. "I'll call you tomorrow, okay?"

"I'll be looking forward to it." *And how!* she added to herself. Then, picking everything up, she stepped onto the escalator, watching him out of the corner of her eye until he was out of sight. It was all she could do to keep from shouting.

* * *

"That went well," Brandon said through a huge grin. "Looks like we have our foot in the door, Mitzi."

CHAPTER 5

Katherine sat staring at the man across the table from her. Was it possible he was really Tanner Nelson? What were the odds of the two of them meeting at the airport the way they had? And to think he'd actually asked her to meet him for lunch! Suddenly the world was a wonderful place, and coming home was all it should be.

Her first night back in Phoenix was certainly not what she had expected it to be. Her plans were to find a room where she could crash to overcome the jet lag and probably sleep in half the next day. But after running into Tanner at the airport and having him say he'd call, sleep suddenly became something very elusive. What little she got came filled with dreams of Tanner, and as far as the sleeping late thing went—she was up at six. By seven she was dressed and beside the phone, waiting and hoping. Would he call, or wouldn't he? Tanner had always been the impatient one, but right now it seemed to have rubbed off on her. By the time he did call, around ten, she was a nervous wreck.

It was impressive the way he remembered her favorite restaurant, the one with the funny name and the greatest Mexican food she'd ever tasted. There was so much Katie had missed about the States those eight years she spent in Melbourne, and one of them was the chile relleno served at Carlos O'Brien's. She wasn't sure what pleased her most at the moment—the wonderful aroma of the restaurant or the company of the ruggedly handsome man just across the table.

"You've cut your hair," Tanner remarked. "I really like it."

"Thanks. My dad hates it. He says a woman is supposed to have long hair. This coming from a man who wore his in a crew cut his whole life."

Tanner changed the subject to one she had been thinking of herself. "What do you think the odds were of coming in on adjoining flights and meeting the way we did at the airport last night?" he asked.

"Pretty darn incredible, I'd say."

"Even more so than you might know," he explained. "If it hadn't been for a certain cabbie having engine trouble on the streets of London yesterday morning, I'd have been home four hours sooner."

Oh my, she mused to herself. *It's almost like the hand of destiny had a part in this.* Since she couldn't see the two angels looking on, she had no way of knowing just how close to the truth her musing was. "What took you to London?" she asked. "Business or pleasure?"

"Business," he responded with a smile. "Out chasing a bad guy."

"I should have guessed. So where did you end up, working for the CIA or something?"

He laughed. "The CIA is too political for my blood, although my job is parallel to what they do at times. But enough about me. Let's talk about you, Katie. How long do you plan on staying in that hotel?"

"No longer than I have to. I want to start apartment hunting in a day or so, just as soon as the jet lag settles down."

"You're going to want something near ASU West, right?"

"The closer the better, since that's where I'll be working."

Tanner folded the menu and set it aside. "You know where my apartment is?" he asked. Without giving her time to answer, he went on. "It's on 43rd Avenue, just south of Thunderbird."

"What? Talk about irony—you're right across the street from ASU West. Are there any openings at your complex?"

He shook his head. "Sorry, Katie. The place stays pretty full, I'm afraid."

"Figures," she said. "Any chance I can talk you into moving out?"

He laughed but let the subject drop. Just then, the server stepped up to see if they were ready to place their order. "I think we're ready," Tanner told him. "I'll have a beef chimichanga, and I'm guessing the lady wants a chile relleno." He looked over at her and grinned.

She smiled back. "Yes, I think I will have a chile relleno. You have a great memory, Mr. Nelson."

"Anything to drink?" the server asked.

"I'll have a lemonade; she wants a Sprite with two straws. Did I get that one right too?" he asked.

"You even remembered the two straws," she laughed. "Always did like drinking with two straws." She was flattered that he remembered something so small. Maybe he did think of her now and then. The server walked away, and Katherine picked up a chip, dipping it in the salsa and biting off the end.

"So tell me about Australia," Tanner suggested. "Is it true they hire kangaroos for bus drivers?"

"No," she laughed. "That's not true. We have lots of kangaroos, though."

"It's funny," Tanner added. "I've pretty much circled the globe in my job, but I've never been to Australia."

She couldn't help but wonder about this. Had he not been to Australia because his job never required him going there, or was it something else? Had he avoided it because he knew she was there? "So what's this job that takes you all over the world?" she asked.

Tanner bit down on a chip. "I'm an investigator for a criminal law firm."

This came as a bit of a shock to Katherine. Being a law firm investigator didn't sound all that exciting. Still, she could be missing something from the title. After all, it was a job that apparently took him all over the world. "So tell me about it," she said. "Does it involve many crime scenes?"

"I get my share of crime scenes," he explained. "But I get a fair share of other things too. Like tracking down certain characters no one else seems able to locate. Tracking them down and bringing them in. That's the fun part." Tanner moved away from the subject of himself and asked a question about her. "You told me you're not married. Is there anyone special in your life?"

Katherine nearly spilled her Sprite when this question came. Her face flushed as she remembered Ned Weathersby. She and Ned had been seeing each other on a fairly regular basis for more than a year now. Ned had proposed, but Katherine had continually put him off. He was a nice enough guy, and one who'd make some woman a great husband, but she just wasn't sure that woman was her. "No," she finally responded. "No one special. I'm not saying I haven't dated, but I must be a little too American for those Aussie blokes."

"Yeah? Those 'blokes,' as you call them, must be either blind or crazy."

Katherine tried to cover her blush. There was no denying her pleasure at Tanner's attention, but letting it show was another matter. When Tanner didn't stop looking, she grabbed another chip and bit into it, doing her best to appear casual. Now it was her turn to change the subject. "I've never heard the full story of what happened to Brandon," she said. "The newscasts didn't reach Melbourne, and I haven't been in touch with anyone stateside for years."

"It's not a very pretty story, I'm afraid. Are you aware that even though Brandon's body was never found, Troy was convicted of his murder?"

"That much I do know, but I don't believe it. Troy and Brandon were inseparable."

"You got that right. Troy was framed by someone with a lot of power. I've never been able to uncover the proof, but I refuse to give up. The real killer had to have made a mistake, Katie. All criminals make mistakes. Once I find that mistake, I will bring the truth to light, and I will see that justice is served."

"How did they convict Troy?" Katherine questioned.

"Through shoddy investigative work, that's how. That, and unethical lawyers. The blood found in Troy's apartment should have been an obvious plant to anyone with a trained eye."

"Brandon's blood?" Katherine guessed.

"It was Brandon's blood, all right. On a handkerchief hidden under the pillow on Troy's sofa. And get this—an anonymous tipster told the police exactly where to look for it. Nothing else was found in the apartment to indicate Brandon had even been there. Nor did Troy have a way to dispose of a body. He didn't own a car. What did he do, wrap the body in a sleeping bag and hitchhike with it over his shoulder to some secluded spot where he could dispose of it?"

Katherine could sense Tanner's frustration over Troy, so when the server showed up with their food, she figured it was a good time to let the subject drop. She had forgotten the size of the portions served at Carlos O'Brien's. She was hungry and it smelled heavenly, but there was no way could she get all that food down. "More drinks?" the server asked, seeing their glasses low.

"Yes, please," Katherine answered. "And could I get more salsa for my chile relleno?"

"Yes, ma'am." The server smiled. "Have it right out."

Katherine sliced off one end of the chile and took a bite. "Oooh, this is even better than I remembered. I think I've died and gone to heaven."

"Enjoy it," Tanner smiled, taking a bite of his chimichanga. "But save room for the fried ice cream." Katherine nodded. She had forgotten about the fried ice cream, but it was something definitely worth saving room for. "I have a suggestion about your apartment problem, Katie," Tanner remarked offhandedly.

She looked up. "What's that?"

"It's kind of a far-out idea, but you might want to consider it. I hold the lease on two adjoining apartments. One of them I live in, the other I've converted into a forensic lab. It would be no trouble at all for me to consolidate into a single apartment. It would be a little crowded, you know, having my living quarters combined with my lab, but it's something I can live with until we can find you a more suitable place."

"Tanner, I can't take your apartment!"

"Hey, it's no big deal. My second apartment has everything I need. Sleeping quarters, a kitchen, the works."

"Tanner . . ."

"What? I'm offering you free rent right across the street from your pending job. You know what they say about a gift horse."

Katherine knew from the look in Tanner's eyes the offer was genuine. Here she was, worried that he might make this one date to Carlos O'Brien's their last and that he might not even call again. Instead he was offering to give up half his living space for her? She didn't know whether to shout for joy, or be embarrassed for even considering the idea. "Tanner, I . . ."

"The apartment's yours, Katie. All you have to do is say the word."

* * *

Two nearby angels stood eagerly watching the lunch date. "Okay, Mitzi," Brandon casually remarked, "I admit you were right in putting the idea about sharing apartments with Katherine in Tanner's mind. And I also admit I never would have thought of it. What I'm trying to say is, you're turning into one great partner."

"Thank you, Brandon. It means a lot to hear you say that."

"So, how are we going to get the two of them moving along into Stage Two of the plan?"

Mitzi knew exactly what Brandon meant by Stage Two, since they had recently discussed the elements of his assignment in detail. The plan entailed getting Tanner back up to Zachary Wagner's cabin, where there was evidence to be uncovered—evidence concerning Brandon's murder, as well as some other things. "I have an idea where to start," she told him. "How about if I plant a dream in Katherine's mind tonight? A haunting dream that she can't shake off until she brings it up to Tanner. When she does bring up the dream, we can take it from there."

"You can plant dreams?" Brandon asked.

"Nothing to it."

"It just might work, Mitzi. Let's do it that way."

CHAPTER 6

Katherine woke to the sound of a mockingbird. For a moment she thought she was back in her room at her folks' old home in Mesa, near the fruitless mulberry tree where the mockingbird family nested every year. As reality surfaced, she shot straight up in bed. She was in Tanner's apartment. No, that didn't sound right. She was in the apartment Tanner had so graciously vacated for her. And what an apartment it was. It had everything, right down to a built-in jacuzzi. She glanced at the closed and locked door separating this apartment from the one Tanner had moved all his things into, and a new fog of guilt settled in as she thought about the sacrifice he was making for her.

It hadn't taken long to move his things out and replace them with what few things she had brought from Melbourne. He had told her his second apartment was converted into a forensic lab, but until she saw it for herself, she had no concept of how complete that lab was. There was equipment the likes of which she had never seen, along with five separate lab tables. He told her he would still have a bedroom and kitchen, and he did—sort of. They were piled high with supplies, but he assured her he could make do. At least the sink, kitchen range, and refrigerator were where he could get to them. That and his bed.

While they were moving his things, she couldn't help but notice the picture he kept on the nightstand next to the bed. It was a picture of the two of them, taken one snowy afternoon at the Flagstaff campus. They had built a snowman, and Tanner had handed the camera to a passerby to snap the picture. Tanner seemed a little embarrassed when he realized Katherine had seen the picture, but she liked the idea of him keeping a reminder of their good times.

Katherine climbed out of bed and pulled on her robe. As she did, a dream she had awakened from lingered in her mind. She had dreamt of a ritual that had first started on a warm spring morning when she and Tanner were students together at NAU. Tanner had been walking her to class that morning, and they were just passing the science building when Katherine felt a sudden urge to remove her shoes and walk the rest of the way barefoot across the lawn. She remembered now how Tanner had laughed at the suggestion, but she chided him into doing it with her. What fools they had made of themselves, but they didn't care. A tradition was born, and they seldom used the sidewalks again. From that morning on, wherever they went on campus together, it was more often than not done barefoot over the lawn. Katherine reasoned it was seeing the picture of her and Tanner in his apartment that had triggered the dream. It was just something silly she hadn't thought of in years.

Once showered and dressed, Katherine looked over her new apartment. She'd be needing several things before she could set up real housekeeping. But she needed to buy a car before she could go shopping. She knew Tanner had to report back to work this morning, but maybe tonight she could ask if he would take her around to a few lots looking for one. She couldn't afford anything new, but she did want something nice. Maybe a Honda Accord.

She heard a rap at the front door and wondered who it could be. She figured it was probably someone looking for Tanner, since the word likely hadn't gotten out that he had moved next door. She stepped to the door and opened it. "Tanner?" She gasped at seeing him. "I thought you went to work."

He grinned. "I reported in by phone, and when I learned there was nothing hot pending, I asked for the day off. I was wondering, would you like to go for some breakfast?"

This brought a memory of another breakfast eight years ago—the one at Denny's. Was Tanner remembering too? "Breakfast sounds nice," she said. "Let me grab my purse."

"I was thinking of Denny's," he said before she had time to step away from the door. "There's one just down the street."

Katherine rolled her eyes but didn't let him see. "Denny's is perfect," she replied.

When she returned with her purse, it was to see him wearing a devilish grin that was a dead giveaway he was on the same wavelength as her with this Denny's thing. "They have great hotcakes and eggs," he said.

She shook her head. "You really do have a remarkable memory, Tanner."

He raised an eyebrow in an attempt to look puzzled. "Memory? About what?"

She stepped out and closed the door behind her. When they reached the restaurant, it was a replay of the previous day's lunch. Tanner did all the ordering himself, and just as she guessed, he set them up with a breakfast exactly the same as the one they had shared that early morning eight years ago.

"So, how'd you sleep last night?" Tanner asked as the server stepped away.

"I slept great. Probably better than you in that cramped room."

"No, no, no—that room's not cramped. You should see some of the places I have to sleep in when I'm on the road. So, what would you like to do today? I have the whole day off, and I'm at your disposal."

"You are unbelievable, Tanner Nelson. First you gave up your room, now you're giving up your day. You're taking all the work out of my coming home."

"Hey, what are old-time friends for? Besides, I have a method to my madness. Once Vincent learns you're home, I may never get another minute alone with you."

The mention of Vincent's name caught Katherine's interest. Of all the men she'd ever known, Tanner, Vincent, and Ned were the only three she'd ever thought of in a romantic way. When she was in college with Tanner and Vincent, she had bounced back and forth between the two so often she sometimes felt like the pendulum on her dad's grandfather clock. In the end it was Tanner who had won her heart, but she wasn't so sure she had ever really let either of them know that for sure. "What's going on with Vincent?" she asked. "Did he ever marry?"

"Vincent? Married? Come on, Katie, what woman in her right mind would ever marry Vincent? Have you forgotten the way he used to hound you for your attention?"

She hadn't forgotten, but she didn't think it would be wise to admit it. "So what's Vincent doing now?" she asked instead.

"Still working for his father, just like always. He wears two hats for the company. He's a vice president as well as his father's personal pilot. Flies the old man all over the world in one of a fleet of company jets. Flies him around in a chopper, too, when the occasion arises."

Katherine knew that Vincent's father was both owner and CEO of Wagner Aerospace, and she had always suspected Vincent would remain with the company. "So what about Cory?" she asked. "Is he still around?"

"You heard Cory talking the whole time you were riding in my car," Tanner laughed.

"I what?"

"The disc jockey on the radio, the one who goes by the name R. L. Dennison. That's our boy Cory."

"Cory's a disc jockey? I thought he wanted to become an actor."

"He got hungry and had to find a way to feed himself until his big break came along. Cory's the only one of the old fivesome who's married. Got himself a great wife. Her name's Stephanie Webber, or it was until she changed it to Stephanie Harper. They met during an audition at a Hollywood studio, where both were trying out for parts in a Disney film. Neither of them got past the interview, but that didn't stop them from taking up with each other and eventually falling in love. They have three daughters, Shelby, Cassandra, and Brittany."

"Cory's a daddy, how fun. Does he still eat like he used to?"

"Nah, you'd never recognize him. Stephanie put him on a diet and got him signed up at a gym."

"You're talking about the same Cory we went to college with?"

"Hard to believe, but true," Tanner assured her.

Katherine sighed. "Sounds like most of our old group ended up doing just fine. If only things had worked out half so well for Brandon and Troy." Katherine wondered if this might be a good time to press Tanner for more details on those two. There probably would never be an ideal time, but this might be as good as any. "I heard Brandon disappeared the same night as the big graduation party," she said.

"Yeah, after I dropped you off that night, I drove home to my apartment in Flagstaff. When I walked in, my answering machine was blinking. I clicked it on to find a message from Brandon. He sounded excited and concerned all at the same time. He told me he'd stumbled onto something big and wanted me to call no matter how late I got in. I tried reaching him for over an hour. I grew more concerned by the minute, so I got back in my car and drove over to his place. It was locked, but I was too impatient to wait for morning, so I picked the lock to find the apartment ransacked. I wasted no time calling the cops."

All this was going on while I lay awake in my bed, crying my eyes out over the way I had decided to tell you good-bye before leaving for Melbourne the next day. My timing couldn't have been worse.

Tanner went on with his explanation. "The next morning we discovered Troy's apartment was under investigation and Troy was nowhere to be found. Once the bloodstained handkerchief turned up, Troy was under immediate suspicion. Two days later, they found Troy walking along Highway 89A, completely out of his mind. There was enough marijuana in his blood to put a horse in never-never land."

"Marijuana?" Katherine gasped. "Troy would never have used marijuana or any other illegal drug."

"Tell me about it. It was all part of the frame. Troy's story was never considered by the prosecution, even though Vincent's story supports it completely. Vincent gave Troy a ride home after the party. The problem was, Vincent drove off before Troy went inside."

"Someone was waiting for him?" Katherine surmised.

"Yeah. They caught him from behind and knocked him out with chloroform. Troy woke up locked and shackled in a dark room. He never got a look at his assailants. They shoved food and water through a hole in the door. He was there two days and refused to eat or drink anything. When he couldn't stand it any longer, he drank the water."

"And that's how he was drugged? With the water?"

"You know that and I know that, but the prosecution refused to accept it. Their contention was Troy got high on his own and murdered Brandon in his drugged state. Troy had little trouble passing three separate lie detector tests, but even those went for nothing. The prosecuting lawyer was a lowlife named Rowan Kentwood. Kentwood saw the chance to get a crime off the books, and to him that took precedence over guilt or innocence. Lying meant nothing to the man. And as for Troy's appeals, Kentwood is the kind who would walk through fire rather than admit he might have made a mistake."

Katherine felt ill just thinking about it. "Where is Troy now?" she asked.

"In the Arizona State Prison at Florence. I try to visit him at least once a month. It's sad seeing him like that. But I have to hand it to the guy, he's overcome his bitterness. He still proclaims his innocence, but he hasn't let prison drag him down. He's actually earned himself a law degree in the years he's been there."

"A law degree. That sounds like Troy. I'm so sorry things worked out the way they did for him. I know he's innocent."

"I'll prove it someday, Katie."

For some reason, last night's dream came back strongly to her mind, and Katherine felt impressed to relate it to Tanner. She shook it off. Telling him about the dream was an outlandish idea. All it would get her was laughed at.

"You never did tell me what you'd like to do with the day," Tanner reminded her. "You might as well take advantage of my being free. Tomorrow I might be off to Italy or who knows where? All part of my job."

"I really hate to . . ."

Tanner held up a hand, cutting her off midsentence. "I'll pretend I didn't hear that," he said. "Now, what was it you wanted to do?"

* * *

"What's the problem?" Brandon pressed. "Why hasn't she mentioned the dream?"

"She's a difficult one, Brandon. But I can reach her, I know I can. Just stand back and give me some operating room. This is going to take every ounce of skill I have."

* * *

"What I really need is someone to help me find a car," Katherine said.

"I can do that. What kind of car do you have in mind?"

"I was thinking maybe a Honda Accord. I hear they're pretty good cars."

"Yeah, they're good cars. I'm sure we can find you one."

The server returned with their breakfast. Katherine picked up a slice of bacon and was about to take a bite when last night's dream came back stronger than ever. What was it about that dream that kept prompting her to mention it to Tanner? Then it hit her. It wasn't just that she wanted to mention the dream to him; she wanted to live the dream. "No," she abruptly said. "I don't want to look for a car. I want to make a run up to Flagstaff. Is that an option on your list of things to do for Katie?"

"Sure, why not?"

"We could just look the place over, you know, for old times' sake. What do you say?"

"Sounds like a plan," Tanner agreed. "It's a beautiful day for a trip to the mountains."

* * *

Mitzi smiled broadly. "There, you see what I can do when I really concentrate?"

"You have them on their way to Flagstaff, I'll give you that, Mitzi. But can you get them out to the cabin where Tanner can find the evidence?"

"Just you wait and see, Brandon Cheney. Just you wait and see."

CHAPTER 7

Katherine was glad Tanner chose the scenic route along Highway 89A that wound its way through Oak Creek Canyon. It had to be one of the prettiest drives in the entire state of Arizona. What made it even better was the little Stingray convertible Tanner now drove. It was a perfect day for a top-down drive. Katherine had to admit, Tanner had come a long way since the days of the old Dodge Neon he once owned.

Not that the Dodge didn't hold a ton of wonderful memories. Between it and Vincent's Porsche, Katherine never wanted for a ride. It was a little immature, she acknowledged with a twinge of regret, the way she deliberately instigated competition between the two of them over whose car she would ride in. But she was young, and being showered with attention from two handsome men was flattering. She just couldn't help it. "So tell me about this car," she said. "Where'd you come across it?"

"You like my car?" he asked with a boyish grin.

"Yes, I love it. Tell me about it."

"Okay. It's a completely restored '69 Corvette Stingray III. It belonged to a drug dealer I helped bust a couple of years back. The car was impounded, and one of the lawyers at the firm where I worked helped me rescue it."

"Cool. So what does Vincent drive now?"

"You know Vince," Tanner laughed. "He thinks the more something costs, the better it is. He's driving a Lexus SC 430. Great car, but the top won't fold down."

"And Vincent's not married?"

"Nope. He almost got married once, but at the last minute, he backed out. Nice lady. She went on to marry one of our local newscasters. They have two kids and appear to be happy campers. Vince still talks about her now and then. He's never been sure whether he made a mistake or not." Tanner glanced over at Katherine. "There's someone else he's never fully gotten over."

"Meaning me?" Katherine asked through a deep blush.

"Meaning you, Katie. Vincent's a good man. If you ever do think of marrying, you could do worse."

Katherine didn't know whether she liked Tanner saying that or not. Not that she didn't think Vincent would make a great husband, and not that she didn't realize she could do worse, but the story Tanner had just told her about Vincent and the other unnamed lady made her realize there was also someone she herself had never completely gotten over—but it wasn't Vincent. She glanced up to see they were just coming to the Flagstaff city limit sign. "The last time I passed that sign, we were headed out of Flag toward my folks' old house in Mesa, remember?"

"How could I ever forget? That was one black day in history for the old gang."

Katherine hadn't meant to open wounds, but that's evidently exactly what her remark had done. Feeling a little guilty, she withdrew into her thoughts. It seemed like another lifetime since she had last been in Flagstaff. The place had grown some, but not all that much. She thought about mentioning a jaunt by the old campus, but didn't have to, as it soon became obvious that was exactly where Tanner was headed. "Believe it or not, this is my first trip back to Flag since I moved out a week after graduation," he said.

This came as a bit of a surprise. Here was a man who traveled all over the world, and yet he hadn't made it far enough to revisit the land of his college days.

* * *

"That really is a great car," Brandon mentioned to Mitzi. "If I'd had one like it when I was a mortal, maybe Katherine would have hit me up for a ride every now and then."

"Yes, and maybe if you'd had a car like that, so many other girls would have been ringing your phone that there would never have been time to give Katherine a ride."

Mitzi was slightly disgusted with herself for saying that. In the first place, she knew Brandon never really was in love with Katherine. The make-believe game of "I Love Katherine" was just that—a game he and his friends used to play. And even if he had been in love with her, why should it matter to Mitzi? It was none of her business. It was certainly stupid to allow herself the hint of jealousy she felt when she saw the way Brandon looked at Katherine. Crazy as it was, she did feel jealous. "If I'm going to entice these two to the cabin," she said, forcing her mind off the subject, "I should look the place over a little closer. All I've seen so far is what you showed me in the hologram."

"You want to see the cabin? You think that'll improve your chances for convincing them to go there?"

"I know it will, and this is the perfect time, while Katherine and Tanner are looking over the old campus."

"Okay, take my hand. Since I know the way, I'll drive."

Mitzi smiled at the way Brandon put it. Angels didn't have to drive. They could do their traveling by simply thinking themselves from one place to the next. Holding Brandon's hand wouldn't help anything, but it was a nice gesture all the same. She touched his hand, and they were instantly there.

"Wow!" Mitzi remarked. "They call this a cabin? I'd call it more of a mountain mansion. This place must be worth a couple million."

"Probably more, but that's just petty cash for Zachary Wagner. It sure is creepy, seeing the old place again. A hologram is one thing, but actually being here . . ."

"Does it bother you because this is where you died?" Mitzi asked.

"I didn't actually die here," Brandon explained. "They shot me, but it was just a superficial wound. The place where I actually died is a long way from this cabin. But this is where it all started, and yes—it is a bit creepy seeing it again. I almost wish I didn't have to go inside."

"I hate to tell you this, but the success of our assignment depends on you going inside, Brandon. It won't be that bad."

"I know. But you have to understand, I was one of those guys who was squeamish seeing my own blood when I cut a finger. Even as an angel, I don't like looking at blood. It's just me, what can I say?"

Mitzi's curiosity was getting the better of her. "If you weren't killed here, where did it happen?"

"It was just a place. I'll take you there sometime, but not today. Maybe after our assignment is in the finished file."

"Sure, but we do need to see inside the cabin. You mentioned Zachary Wagner—I take it he still owns the place?"

"Yeah. He uses it to entertain prospective clients. I understand he's upped the security a notch since my little antic. And he's much more careful how he uses the computer now."

"Upped the security? That might make it difficult for Tanner and Katie to get inside."

"Don't kid yourself, Mitzi. Tanner can handle whatever security Zachary Wagner has installed. You should know that if you've been tagging along with him the past five years."

"You're right, I just wasn't thinking. So where exactly are these clues we're supposed to lead him to?"

"In Wagner's office where I broke into his computer eight years ago. There are two clues. One, I left on purpose, the other was anything but my doing."

From the way Brandon said this, Mitzi thought she knew his meaning. "Your blood?" she guessed.

"My blood. I told you I was shot."

"That was eight years ago, Brandon. Would there be any trace left by now?"

"Oh, yeah. Blood is hard to hide from someone as skilled as Tanner. Even eight-year-old blood. He'll use what's called a Luminol test."

Mitzi was familiar with the Luminol test, as she had seen Tanner use it before. She also knew that Tanner kept a case in his Stingray with all the necessary equipment to perform the test. She still wasn't sure that traces of Brandon's blood would be there after all these years, but she didn't mention it a second time. Instead, she got back to the business at hand. "I'm ready to see that office now. Shall we go in?"

CHAPTER 8

Katherine and Tanner stood on the edge of the campus lawn, gazing across at the buildings on the far side. "Are you thinking what I'm thinking?" she ventured.

"A barefoot walk across the grass?"

"You remembered," she said.

"Only like it was yesterday. Are you game?"

"What do you think?" she asked, pulling off her shoes. "Come on, I'll race you to the other side."

Even with her head start, she knew Tanner would catch up before they reached the middle of the lawn. He didn't disappoint her. When they reached the other side, he grasped her arm and brought them both to a stop. "Remember the first day we ever did this?" he asked.

"How could I not? That was the day I lost my physics homework and got a failing grade from Professor Hunter. You remember Hunter, the teacher?"

"I remember Hunter, but I also remember better things about that day."

"Like our first barefoot walk across this lawn?" she said, grinning. "I remember that too. Those walks were great fun, weren't they? What ever happened to that boy and girl, Tanner? How did they ever grow into us?"

Tanner laughed but didn't respond. Katherine almost told him about her dream right then and had to bite her lip to keep silent. They started walking again and met a group of students going the opposite way. "Look," she said. "They have their shoes off. Our tradition is still alive."

"They look out of place," Tanner remarked. "They're just not the right faces."

"Yes, they are. They're the faces of today. The faces you remember are the ones from yesterday."

"Maybe so, but these faces look so young."

"So did ours, Tanner. Because we were young."

"You were," he laughed. "I don't think I was ever young. I've always been this old."

"Is that a hint that you see me as old?"

Tanner's face turned red, bringing an amused grin to Katherine's. "No, I didn't . . . That is . . ." He paused for a breath. "Katie Dalton, I've never seen you more beautiful than you are right now. Not to say you weren't beautiful then, but you're even more so now."

It suddenly became Katherine's turn to blush. "Thank you," she said, her voice softened by the emotion his remark suddenly stirred in her.

"So, what do you want to do after we're finished looking over the campus?" Tanner asked. "We could rent a couple of horses and go for a ride in the woods."

"Tanner," she laughed, "I've been living on a ranch in Melbourne for the past eight years. Sorry, but I've had all the horses I can stand for a while."

"Let me ask you something," Tanner said, changing the subject. "Do you believe in angels?"

"What?" she asked. "Why would you ask that?"

"I don't know. I've just been having some feelings lately."

"What kind of feelings?"

Tanner brushed a hand over his mouth and shifted his weight nervously. Katherine knew he wanted to tell her something, but he apparently didn't know how to do it. "Just feelings," he said. "Like now, for instance. I've got a feeling Brandon's nearby."

Katherine paused for a moment. "You know, now that you bring it up, I feel the same way too."

Tanner shook his head. "This is crazy. Brandon can't be here."

"Why can't he?" Katherine asked. "You asked if I believe in angels—well, I do! And I believe Brandon is an angel now. He could be here with us, if he wanted to."

"You really think?"

"Yes, I do. And I not only think he's here with us, I think he's trying to tell us something."

Tanner exhaled. "Like maybe chastising me for never solving his murder?"

"Maybe more than that, Tanner. Think about this. What if Brandon, as an angel, wanted the two of us team up and work on solving his murder? What if he even had something to do with us meeting at the airport the way we did?"

Tanner eyed her skeptically. "I'm a man who deals with factual evidence, not the whisperings of an apparition."

"You're the one who brought the subject up."

"I just feel like Brandon is here and that he's trying to tell me something about his murder."

"So do I," Katherine said. "Do you know what gave me the idea for coming to Flagstaff? It was a dream. Last night I dreamed we were walking barefoot across this lawn, just like we're doing now."

"You did?"

"Yes, I did."

"And you think Brandon had something to do with you dreaming that?"

"Maybe."

Tanner turned silent and remained that way for several seconds. When at last he spoke, it was with a suggestion that caught Katherine's complete attention. "I want to drive up to Zachary Wagner's cabin, Katie. I don't know why, but I think Brandon wants us to look the place over."

"Well then, we'd better be off."

* * *

"It worked!" Brandon shouted. "You whispered to them, and they heard!"

Mitzi felt herself suddenly swept into Brandon's arms, where she was crushed into a hug. "You're terrific!" Brandon yelled so loud it stung Mitzi's ear, only inches from his lips. "How would I have ever done this without you?" He backed away, but stood looking at her, still smiling. "Do we make a great team or what?"

Mitzi hadn't realized that as an angel, she was still capable of having her breath taken away, but it was just what Brandon's hug had done to her. Somehow, she didn't mind. In fact, she liked it. "We do make a good team, don't we?" she agreed, a little shocked at just how strongly she had managed to reach both Tanner and Katherine. She wasn't about to admit it to Brandon, but she strongly suspected someone with a lot more authority than her was behind this one. It was just too convenient the way they both concluded what they did about going to the cabin.

* * *

"I'll scope out the cabin," Tanner proposed, "after I get you checked into a room where you can wait for me."

"You'll do no such thing! I feel just as strongly about checking that cabin as you do, and I'm not about to be shoved aside."

"Be reasonable, Katie. This is what I do. This kind of stuff is second nature to me, but I won't have you subjected to those same dangers. You'll be safe in a hotel room."

Katherine shook her head vigorously. "Let's get one thing straight right here and now—you are not my father! And even if you were, I'm way past the point of being bossed around! I will not wait in a room. I will check out the cabin right alongside you!"

From Tanner's stunned look, Katherine knew he wasn't used to being talked to that way. She didn't care. She had said exactly what she felt, and she meant it—every word of it.

Tanner walked a few steps away and stood deep in thought. Then, slowly, he turned to face her. "I want your promise you'll do exactly what I say."

"Just as long as what you say has nothing to do with keeping me out of the action."

He sighed. "Agreed. Come on, let's get started."

CHAPTER 9

Tanner had been driving north on Highway 89 for about half an hour after leaving Flagstaff when the turnoff to Zachary Wagner's multimillion dollar cabin came into view. The cabin was situated several hundred feet off the road, completely surrounded by a majestic stand of ponderosa pines. Tanner pulled off the highway and came to a stop at the entrance to the private road. Without a word of explanation, he got out and spent several minutes looking things over. Katherine hadn't a clue what he was doing, but she figured he was the expert in such things. When he got back in the car, he turned to her. "Do you still keep a journal, Katie?"

"Every day, without fail."

Tanner shoved his foot down and the car lunged forward. "Pray tonight's entry won't be all that exciting." That wasn't the most comforting thing he might have said, but she wasn't going to let it show.

At the cabin, the road ended in a circle right outside the front entrance. There was parking off to one side, which Tanner ignored. He pulled right up to the house and shut off the engine. "The place doesn't look much different," he observed. "A coat of fresh paint maybe. Some of the shrubs are bigger."

Katherine had only been to the cabin a limited number of times, the last being the night of the party. She agreed that it didn't look all that different from the way she remembered it. "Move over to the driver's seat," Tanner instructed as he stepped out. "I want to have a look around to see what we're up against. If anything goes wrong—anything at all—I want you to beat a path out of here. Don't stop until you reach Flag, then head straight for the police station. Got that?"

"Yeah, sure, like I'd leave you here."

"Don't get in a quandary over me, Katie. I can handle myself. Just do as I say."

Katherine rounded the car and slid in behind the wheel. "I'm not sure what kind of security to expect," Tanner went on to explain. "Hopefully, a mountain cabin won't be high enough on Wagner's list of priorities to use anything too sophisticated." Tanner reached in the backseat and removed a black leather case. "Cop stuff," he told her, evidently reading the unasked question in her eyes.

"Cop stuff," she echoed, watching him walk away. He disappeared behind the house, and she suddenly felt very much alone. She glanced around nervously but noticed nothing out of the ordinary. "Stay in the car," she told herself. "That's what Tanner said. Stay in the car."

For the first time it struck her that what they were doing wasn't exactly legal. They really should have a search warrant for this sort of thing. Still, if Zachary Wagner did have something to hide inside the cabin, a search warrant wouldn't be the way to go. In the first place, how could they get a warrant based on the evidence that they both felt a departed friend urging them here? Added to that would be the fact that whatever they were looking for hadn't been discovered in the past eight years. "Oh, boy," she moaned. "Legal or not, I guess this is the only way to go."

From somewhere in the overhead branches, a pinecone fell, bouncing noisily off the hood of the Stingray. "That's it," she exclaimed, grabbing her purse and the car keys. "I think Tanner needs my help a little closer than here." Jumping from the car, she hurried around the house, where she spotted Tanner at an electrical panel.

"What are you doing?" Tanner snapped as she hurried up. "I told you to stay in the car!"

"You did?" she asked through a sheepish grin. "I must not have heard you right. I thought you said don't leave the keys in the car. I didn't. Here they are." She handed him the keys.

Tanner let out a frustrated breath, took the keys, and slid them into his pocket. Then he pulled a set of latex gloves from the black leather case. "Put these on," he said. "And from here on out, do exactly as I say!"

"Exactly as you say, right." She pulled the gloves on, seeing Tanner had already done the same.

Tanner went back to checking the electrical panel. "I'm surprised," he said. "Either Wagner feels he has nothing here to hide or he doesn't understand high-tech security. The security in this place has holes big enough to drive a truck through. I'd have more trouble getting into Mom's old cookie jar than here."

"What's with the electrical box?" Katherine asked.

"This top part is the panel feeding electrical power to the whole cabin. The smaller part, at the bottom, is the controls for the security system, such as it is."

As Katherine looked on, Tanner opened the cover and applied a set of jumpers taken from his bag to some terminals inside. "This system works on heat sensors," he explained. "The cabin will be laced with sensors in every room. If any one sensor detects body heat, a little transmitter in this box sends a signal to a remote location where security is being constantly monitored. What I've done here will defeat the transmitter. The sensors will still know we're inside, but they can't tell anyone."

"So, how do we get inside?" she asked.

"Through the front door. How else?" Tanner removed a set of picks from his bag. "I have a master key." He grinned.

They rounded the cabin to the front door, and Tanner had it unlocked in a matter of seconds. He pushed it open and made a thorough scan of the inside. Katherine peeked over his shoulder to see for herself. Not much had changed on the inside either. From the cleanliness of the place, it was obvious Zachary had someone looking after it on a regular basis. "Okay, we're in," she anxiously whispered. "What now?"

"Now we try to retrace Brandon's steps from the last time we saw him the night of the party."

She thought a moment. "The last I remember seeing Brandon, he was standing next to the punch bowl, which was on a table right over there next to that wall."

"That's the way I remember it too. You and I were with him, and so was Cory. Brandon showed us the watch his grandfather had given him, then coaxed me to get you out on the dance floor when he noticed Vince walking up."

Katherine had forgotten about Brandon doing that, but she did remember dancing a short time with Tanner before pressuring him into leaving the party so they could get an early start down the hill. "From the time we left Brandon at the punch bowl until we left the party was twenty minutes, tops," she remarked.

"Yeah, and when we did leave, Brandon was nowhere in sight. I distinctly remember looking around for him. Cory and Vince were still near the punch bowl, and by that time Troy had joined them. But no Brandon."

"I remember something!" Katherine suddenly blurted out. "I glanced at the stairs and saw Brandon going up them. I remember thinking he shouldn't be doing that; it was strictly against Vincent's orders."

"You saw Brandon climbing the stairs?" Tanner asked excitedly.

"Yes. I hadn't thought about that again until just now, but I did see him on the stairs. I'm certain of it. But why would he ignore Vincent's warning about going up there?"

"That's a good question," Tanner remarked. "Maybe the answer lies somewhere upstairs now. Let's have a look."

"Have you ever seen the upstairs?" Katherine asked.

"No. Vince was always protective of that part of the cabin."

"Well, I have."

"You've what?" Tanner gasped. "When?"

Katherine struggled for the right way to phrase what she was about to say. "You weren't the only guy I ever dated back in our college days," she soberly began. "I did go out with some others, you know."

"I knew that."

The inflection in Tanner's voice was a dead giveaway that this part of the conversation was not all that comfortable for him. Katherine couldn't help slyly wondering why, but she chose to ignore it and continue. "Once, when Vincent and I were on an afternoon drive, he got a call from his father."

"You were on an afternoon drive with Vince?" Tanner responded, evidently missing the part about the call from Vincent's father.

"Yes, I went for a drive with Vincent. Was there a law against that?"

A foolish look crossed Tanner's face as the realization of his reaction struck him. "No, of course not," he responded. "Vincent's father called? About what?"

"About a phone number. Zachary had scribbled the number on a pad in his office, and he needed it right away. He asked Vincent to stop by the cabin and get the number, then call it back to him."

"You were in Zachary's office?"

"I was, and I know exactly where it is."

"Was there a computer there?"

Katherine knew where this question was headed. Brandon was a computer nut through and through. If something tempted him to go against Vincent's warning about upstairs, what greater lure would there be than a computer? "Yes!" she half shouted. "There was a computer!"

Tanner glanced again at the stairs. "Show me the room," he said.

Katherine saw her chance for some fun, and she took it. "I will just as soon as you admit having me along is helpful."

"Katie," he pleaded.

She folded her arms. "Stop being so stubborn and admit it."

"I'm not being stubborn; I'm being sensible. I am not a stubborn man."

She broke out laughing. "I hate to be the one to break this to you, Mr. Perfect, but you are stubborn. When you get something into your head, a steam locomotive couldn't drag it out. Now admit it! My knowing about the office is a big help."

"I could find the office on my own."

"You wouldn't even have thought about it if I hadn't remembered seeing Brandon going upstairs."

Tanner rolled his eyes. "Okay, I admit it. You're a big help. Now, which room is Zachary's office?"

Katherine started up the stairs. It was a little victory, but it felt good, and it helped calm her anxiety about being here illegally. "There," she said, reaching the top of the stairs. "Down the hall, last room on the right."

It was almost frightening the way Tanner had the lock picked as fast as most people could use a key. The inside of the room had changed some since she had last seen it, but not much. The computer was obviously a newer model, but it was on the same desk where the old one had been. And the desk was in the same place. She reached for the light switch. "No!" Tanner said, grabbing her hand. "The lights could be rigged to set off a secondary alarm."

Katherine felt a rush of uneasiness. "I thought you said you had the thing disarmed."

"I disarmed the primary alarm. There could be a secondary alarm tied to things like light switches. The secondary alarm would be a noisemaker, like a siren—something we can definitely do without. I'll raise the blinds. We'll have to do with what light that gives us."

After raising the blinds, Tanner's next stop was the computer. "I'm betting this is where Brandon disappeared to," he remarked. "If he knew there was a computer here, the party would have been pushed to the back burner. Even if Zachary had his computer password protected, Brandon could have been in it faster than it would take him to spell his name backward."

"Are you thinking he might have discovered something on the computer to put his life in danger?"

"Yes, and so are you. It's the most logical solution."

"So you're hinting that Zachary Wagner might be a suspect in your book?" Katherine asked.

"I am. I think Zachary has secrets hidden away so deep they've never seen the light of day. I've always had a bad feeling about Zachary Wagner, but I've kept it to myself for Vincent's sake. I really can't understand how Vince can be so blind as not to see it himself. But Vince thinks the sun rises and sets on his father. He'd never believe the man could do any wrong. It almost makes me wonder if . . ."

Tanner's unfinished sentence sent a spike of concern through Katherine's mind. "You're not hinting you suspect Vincent of any wrongdoing?" she gasped.

Tanner shook his head. "You don't know how much I want to believe otherwise."

"But you're trained to think a certain way?" she guessed.

"Something like that, Katie." Tanner removed a spray bottle and a battery-operated light from his bag. "Let's take a look to see if there might be some secret hidden away in here that a Luminol test could uncover."

Katherine was confused. "Shouldn't you start by checking the computer?"

"Two reasons for not doing that. First, it's not the same computer. And second, I'm guessing this computer is connected to a network. If I were to power it up, chances are it could alert someone at another station."

"Is it possible that might have happened to Brandon?"

"Brandon was an expert on electronics, and he would never have missed the possibility of being detected that way. But he might have been so engrossed in the challenge of breaking into the computer that he overlooked something."

* * *

"How am I doing?" Mitzi asked excitedly.

"You're doing fantastic!" Brandon assured her. "Next, you have to get Tanner over to that wall with the Luminol spray. "That's where he'll find my . . . you know."

"Yes, I know."

"I hid a computer disk there too, one with enough information to hang Zachary Wagner out to dry. Look, right there in the crack between those two logs. See it?"

"Yes, I do see it. You're darn lucky it's never been found in all these years."

"It's pretty well hidden, and I suspect the authorities had something to do with it staying that way. Now all you have to do is get Tanner to notice it."

Mitzi studied the situation carefully. Tanner was right in front of the computer, about three feet from where he needed to be. She still wasn't sure Brandon's blood would show up after all these years, but why should she doubt? If the computer disk had remained hidden all that time, maybe Brandon was right about some celestial help being involved. "All right, Mr. Nelson," she said. "I know you don't believe in me, but that's never stopped you from listening to my suggestions. I want you to concentrate on that wall to your left. There's something hidden there you need to find. Part of it you can find with that Luminol spray. Now, get to it."

* * *

Tanner removed the top on the spray bottle and pressed off a few shots at the area surrounding the computer. Switching on the blue light, he slowly moved it in a circle, working his way outward. He sprayed again and moved even farther back, inching his way through the entire section of the room. "Here!" he suddenly said, pointing to a faint glow. "My hunch was right."

Katherine moved in for a closer look. She felt ill just thinking this might be traces of Brandon's blood. "Can you get a good enough sample for a DNA test?" she asked.

"Oh, yeah. With the equipment I have in my lab I can." Tanner glanced up, smiling faintly at her. "This could come as a shock, Katie, but I have DNA samples filed away for my friends, including Brandon. You never know when my samples might come in handy. Like now, for instance."

"You keep DNA samples?" she gasped. "On me too?"

"Yeah. Along with your fingerprints and a sample of your hair. I take my occupation seriously."

"You have samples on me? How did you . . . ?"

"Hey, it was a snap. Hair from your comb when you didn't notice, prints from some movie tickets, and DNA from . . ."

"From where?" she demanded.

"Well, if you'll remember, you did kiss me on more than one occasion."

"Lipstick? You got my DNA from my lipstick? You used me, Tanner Nelson! I would never have kissed you if I'd known that was your intention." It was a lie, but she didn't want him to know it.

Tanner went to work gathering samples of the blood. He was just finishing when something else caught his eye on the wall next to him. "What have we here?" he asked, digging the computer disk out from between the logs.

"A computer disk?" Katherine said, realizing even in her untrained mind what this could mean.

"This was obviously hidden here on purpose, I'm guessing by the same person who fell here after being shot."

"You think if Brandon did find something he might have copied it to a disk before being confronted by Zachary's men?"

"That's exactly what I'm thinking, Katie. If someone shot Brandon and he fell next to the wall, he may well have hidden the disk without being seen. It was crammed in there far enough that I barely noticed, even with my face right next to it."

Katherine suddenly noticed a beeping sound coming from Tanner's pocket. "What's that?" she asked.

Tanner removed the gadget from his pocket and shut it off. "That's a signal we have trouble. It's time for a hasty exit, Katie. We're about to have company."

"What?" she gasped. "How do you know?"

"When I got out of the car at the entrance to the private road, I set up a motion detector just in case. Well, guess what?"

"Someone is headed for the cabin?"

"Looks like. We have to move fast. You go to the car and get it started. I'll grab my jumpers off the security panel to cover our tracks, then join you."

Katherine didn't want to split up, but she knew Tanner was right—this was the best way. Taking the keys from him, she ran for the car. She started it, just like he had asked, but then moved to the passenger side with the idea of leaving the driving to him. Tanner showed up just seconds later. The car was in motion even before his door slammed closed.

"Are we going to try and outrun them?" Katherine asked, realizing they would be spotted on their way out.

"No need for that," Tanner replied. "I know another way out. If we're lucky, we'll be out of sight before they arrive. Hang on, you're in for a rough ride."

Katherine held her breath as the Stingray headed straight for a stand of ponderosa pines in the opposite direction of the road that brought them there. "Are you sure about this?" she gulped as the car snaked between two pines without room for a playing card on either side.

"I'm sure. If Vince's Porsche could do this, I know darn well my Stingray can. Vince and I discovered this back way out one night trying to ditch a guy after Vince made a pass at his girlfriend."

Katherine closed her eyes and said a silent prayer as the Stingray jostled, bounced, and swerved over places she was sure a car was never meant to go. At last they burst out of the trees and sped onto the wonderfully flat surface of Highway 89. Tanner headed for Flagstaff with the pedal to the floor.

"What about your motion detector?" Katherine called out as they sped past the private road.

"Leave it! It's not worth getting caught. I'm not sure what we've stumbled onto here, Katie, but you can bet it's something Zachary Wagner and his gang wouldn't want us seeing. I want to get this stuff back to my lab where I can check it out."

Katherine suddenly realized that her "relaxing" day at Flagstaff was over. It had taken a sinister turn into the unexpected. Were they really on to something that might reveal Brandon's true fate? All she could do was hope.

CHAPTER 10

Conrad Donahue eased the dark green Cadillac to a stop directly in front of Zachary Wagner's cabin. He stepped from the car and removed his sunglasses. He slowly scanned the area, looking for anything out of the ordinary. On the surface, everything seemed normal, but a gut feeling told him otherwise. After one last glance around to be sure he was alone, he headed straight for the security panel, where he removed the cover and examined everything closely. To the naked eye there was no evidence of tampering, but he knew the diagnostic test would tell the real story. Conrad removed a small electronic device from his blazer pocket and punched in the code while watching a series of lights visually track the system's status. The system seemed to be working perfectly now, but the same test performed remotely less than half an hour earlier had indicated a serious problem. He dropped to one knee and examined the soft earth beneath the panel. Fresh footprints there gave rise for concern.

Conrad next moved to the front of the cabin and found the door locked. Using his key, he opened it and stepped inside. Nothing in this part appeared to be out of place, but he still felt something was askew, and he wasn't about to back off until he discovered what it was.

He glanced at the stairs, remembering the trouble that had once occurred in Zachary's office. Was it possible history was repeating itself? Cautiously, he climbed the stairs, remaining alert to any possible surprises along the way. Pausing at the office door, he listened for any sound. Complete silence. He gripped the knob and gave it a twist. It was securely locked, just the way he'd left it when he was here with his partner, Franco, two hours earlier.

Very quietly, he slid a key in the lock, then pushed the door open a crack. He instantly knew something was out of place. The window blinds had been opened, allowing extra light to enter the room. He had checked those blinds not two hours ago. Someone had been in this room since that time.

Conrad was furious. The security people had swept down the entire cabin not five hours before and had declared it clean at that time. Now it would have to be swept down again, and there wasn't much time since the cabin was scheduled for a business conference in the early evening hours. This would be a maximum-security-level meeting since it included several high-ranking military officers.

Conrad could kick himself for not staying at the cabin after the sweep down. Since he and Franco were planning to remain at the cabin throughout the time of the meeting, which probably wouldn't break up until the early hours of the morning, they had decided it wouldn't hurt to slip away to a local club for drinks and a hand or two of poker. They had ample time to get back before any of the guests would arrive—several hours, in fact. Wagner wouldn't be happy when he learned of a security breach while Conrad and Franco were away playing.

Everything had seemed fine until Conrad decided to run a remote test on the cabin's security system. That's when he'd discovered the problem. The test had indicated a system's transmitting device failure. He grabbed Franco and came right to the cabin, leaving Franco at the entrance to the private road. He wanted him in position to get a look at anyone exiting the premises.

Conrad's cell phone sounded. "Yeah, what do you have?" Conrad asked.

"Plenty on this end," Franco shot back. "I found a motion detector. Someone was expecting you at the cabin."

"That explains their hurried exit," Conrad reasoned. "We did have visitors, but there's no sign of them now, and there was no sign of them on the road either. They must have found another way out."

"Straight through the woods," Franco confirmed. "I got a fix on 'em when they hit the highway. They were in a red sports car. There was guy driving, and a woman passenger."

"Did you get pictures?"

"Yeah. I got shots of the occupants, and I got the license plate."

"Good work, Franco. Did either of them see you?"

"No, I made sure of that."

"I want to do some more looking around here. Give Zachary a call and let him know what we found. He'll want to run a trace on that license plate, and he'll want to contact our people to run another check on the cabin."

"I'm on it."

Shoving the phone back into his pocket, Conrad went over the office inch by inch, turning up nothing more than an unusual chemical smell. That had him worried, especially since it was something he couldn't identify. Leaving the cabin, he continued checking the outside. Where the driveway pavement met forest just east of the cabin, he found tire tracks leading toward the highway. "That's how they got away, all right," he reasoned aloud. "But we've got 'em."

CHAPTER 11

Vincent was just buttoning things up at the hangar after a round trip flight to Denver in one of the company jets. He had flown there to pick up a couple of military brass and return them to Phoenix to discuss a multimillion-dollar contract with Wagner Aerospace. These men were scheduled to ride up to the Flagstaff cabin with Zachary in his limousine later in the day. At the cabin, they'd meet with a group of engineers from the firm to cover a few details of the program in question. Zachary's chauffeur met the men when Vincent landed not twenty minutes ago. They were checking into a hotel now.

Vincent slipped a key into the desk in his office and locked it. He headed for the door with the intention of driving straight home. He hadn't gotten three steps when his cell phone rang. A glance revealed it was Cory Harper. "Yeah, Cory, what's up?" Vincent responded.

"I'll tell you what's up!" Cory instantly shot back. "Our boy Tanner is pulling a fast one, that's what's up."

"Tanner?" Vincent laughed. "What's he up to that could possibly interest me?"

"Would you believe Katherine's back in town?"

"Katie?" Vincent excitedly responded. "Are you kidding? She's here?"

"I thought that would pique your interest. She flew in from Australia day before yesterday. Tanner met her at the airport and is busy keeping her all to himself. One of the guys here at the station spotted them near the escalator. I just learned about it an hour ago when he showed up for work after his two days off."

Vincent quickly considered this. "Tanner knew she was flying in and kept it to himself?"

"Wait till you hear the rest of it. I put out the word over the airwaves for my listeners to watch for a bright red, vintage 1969 Corvette Stingray III with a man and a blond woman inside. I told them it was a contest. Anyone spotting the car and giving me an exact location got their name in a drawing for tickets to the upcoming George Strait concert."

Vincent rolled his eyes. "Sneaky," he responded. "Did it work?"

"Sure it worked! My lines have been ringing off the hook. Tanner and Katherine are headed south on Interstate 17 about thirty miles this side of Flag even as we speak."

"He took her to Flag? Why would he take her up there?"

"Don't know, Vince. But they're on their way home now, it would seem. I used my expertise finding them, so now it's your turn. I can't get involved, naturally, being a married man and all. But I doubt you're of a mind to let this pass."

"You got that right, Cory. Thanks for the heads-up. I owe you a big one. Can you keep me posted as to their exact location?"

"I can do better than that. I just talked to a friend of mine from the sheriff's office. He's off duty and owes me a big favor. Listen up, Vince, while I tell you what I have working."

Vincent couldn't help laughing after he heard Cory's plan. "I'm proud of you, man," he told Cory. "That's a classic. That beats anything I might have come up with."

"Just because I'm married doesn't mean I've lost my touch, Vince. And you owe me a minute-by-minute description of what comes down tonight."

"You got it. Thanks, big guy. This is going to be great fun."

Vincent shut off his phone. "So Katie's here in Arizona?" he said to himself. "Would you ever believe . . . ? And Tanner thinks he has her all to himself." Vincent grinned. "You're in for a surprise, my man. A great big surprise."

* * *

Katherine understood how anxious Tanner was to get back to his lab to check this newly discovered evidence, so it didn't surprise her in the least when he bypassed the scenic route for I-17 on the way home. They were barely out of Flagstaff when the deejay, whom she now knew was Cory, announced a radio contest. "This is R. L. Dennison speaking, and have I got a deal cooking for you! How do tickets to George Strait sound? I have two of them here I'm just dying to give away."

"There's Cory again," she remarked.

"Yep, that's Cory," Tanner replied. "Trying to give something away, as usual."

Cory continued. "We've got a little game going, people. In case you haven't heard, we have a mystery car hidden somewhere within the sound of my voice, and it's up to you to find our car and pinpoint its location. That's all you have to do to get your name in a drawing for two George Strait tickets. Sound easy? That's the way we like our games to work."

"Mystery car?" Tanner laughed. "Now there's a hot one. What'll he think of next?"

"Everybody listen up, because I'm about to repeat the description of our mystery car. Remember, it could be anywhere within the sound of my voice. It may be parked someplace, it may be roaming a city street, or it could even be on a jam-packed freeway. That's all part of the fun. But, this car won't be hard to spot. I think you'll agree when you learn what it is."

"Uh-oh," Tanner moaned as the first hint of what Cory was up to crossed his mind. "I think we're about to become instant celebrities, Katie."

Katherine glanced over at Tanner. "What?"

Tanner motioned toward the radio as Cory continued. "What you're looking for is a candy-apple red, 1969 Corvette Stingray III, possibly with a man and a blond woman inside. How many of those do you see on the road today? I said it would be easy, and I wasn't lying, was I? Keep an eye out and let me know what you see. That's all it takes to have your name in a drawing for two George Strait tickets. And you heard it from the one and only R. L. Dennison."

"That's us!" Katherine laughed. "What's that nut up to?"

"That nut has learned you're home, Katie. We now have listeners all over the state just dying to tell him where to find us. And you can bet Vince won't be far behind them."

"Vincent? You think?"

"I know. There's no way we can make it home with those two bent on finding us."

That was the most ridiculous thing Katherine had ever heard. "Aren't you exaggerating some?" she asked. "Even if they do know where we are, how could they keep us from driving straight home?"

"Elementary, my dear Katie. With Cory's friends in every walk of life and Vince's ingenuity to back him up, there's no stopping those guys. And you can bet whatever they come up with will be pretty darn dramatic."

Katherine laughed. "I think you're blowing this all out of proportion."

"I wish I could agree, Katie. But I'm betting against you."

For the next hour, the subject never surfaced again. Still, Katherine couldn't help noticing how edgy Tanner was, constantly checking his rearview mirror as well as the cars in the opposite lane. They were just approaching the final rest stop before reaching Phoenix when Tanner uttered an abrupt, "Uh-oh! I think it's show time, Katie."

Seeing him glance in his mirror, she turned for a look. To her surprise, she spotted an unmarked patrol car with the lights flashing. She was certain Tanner hadn't been speeding, so she was mystified as to the reason he was being pulled over.

"The guy wants me to pull off at the rest stop," Tanner said. "This has Cory Harper written all over it."

"You're really hung up on this thing, aren't you?" Katherine said. "It's silly, you know. Cory wouldn't do such a thing, and neither would Vincent."

"Then why is this cop on my tail?"

"I don't know. But not because of what you're thinking."

"I have little choice but to pull over; the cop is probably real enough. But if you see a chopper head in as soon as I'm stopped, you can bet Vincent is the pilot. They couldn't have picked a worse time for their little game. I need to get to my lab."

Tanner pulled off at the rest stop with the patrol car right behind. Katherine felt her heart speed as she heard the sound of an approaching helicopter. Was there a chance Tanner was right?

"In case you hadn't noticed," Tanner pointed out, "That's a chopper closing in."

"I don't understand. Why would those guys do this?"

"'Those guys' will be narrowed down to Vincent in a minute, Katie. I suspect the cop was Cory's doing, but he won't take things any further than a married man should. As for the why? Think about it. With my great looks and sparkling personality, would Vincent want the competition? He figures I've had my chance alone with you; now it's his turn."

"You really think so?" Katherine asked anxiously.

"I really do. I'm sorry to leave you in his clutches, Katie, but you know as well as I do he's harmless. I figure it'll go something like this. I'll be handcuffed and given my rights. The charges could be anything from a suspected drug bust to stealing my own car. That's when Vince will swoop in from the sky to carry you off on the wings of his daddy's chopper. Under different circumstances, I'd find a way to foil his plot, but that could tie up my whole evening, and I need to get to that lab. You'll be all right. He'll probably take you out for a great evening, then bring you home late. Knock on my door when you get in. I'll still be up running tests."

"But what if the officer takes you to jail or something?"

"Leave that to me, Katie. Just go with the flow and show Vincent a fantastic time. He deserves it for what it'll cost him later."

Katherine held her breath as the officer approached on Tanner's side. "Please step out of the car," he said in a commanding voice.

Tanner winked at Katherine, then turned back to the officer. "What's the problem? I know I wasn't speeding."

"Out of the car," the officer commanded.

"I can do that, officer. But first I want to hear the charge. What did Cory and Vince tell you to use as an excuse for this bust?"

Katherine noticed the officer trying to hide a surprised reaction. "You're wanted on an outstanding warrant for driving on an expired license," the officer said, his voice less demanding this time.

"Driving on an expired license?" Tanner laughed. "That's the best those guys could come up with? I should at least rate armed robbery."

Before the officer could respond, Tanner opened his door, stepped out, and assumed a spread-eagle position, leaning against the hood of his car. He even went so far as to put his hands behind his back, making the officer's job easy. For a moment, the officer remained frozen, but then stepped in and applied the cuffs. Moving to the patrol car, he opened the back door for Tanner, who got inside. The officer closed the door and headed back in Katherine's direction just as the chopper set down not twenty feet away. "Are you Katherine Dalton?" the officer asked.

"Yes, I'm Katherine."

"I'm sorry you had to be put through this, ma'am, but there's a friend of yours here to pick you up."

"Vincent Wagner?" she guessed, causing the officer another start.

"Mr. Wagner says you know him, is that right?"

"Know him well, officer."

"He offered to pick you up so you don't have to go down to the jail with Mr. Nelson."

Katherine grabbed her purse and stepped out of the car. The officer then escorted her over to the waiting chopper. On the way, she glanced at Tanner to see him holding up a pair of open handcuffs and a wallet. He winked at her, and she couldn't help but laugh. Tanner had picked the officer's pocket and the man didn't even know it yet.

"Katie!" Vincent shouted over the noise of the chopper as she came to the door. "What a sight for sore eyes! Get in!"

She did with the officer's help. He closed her door, and she snapped the seat belt.

"Katie, Katie, Katie," Vincent said, moving the controls to lift the chopper off. "What are you doing in Arizona?"

"I've come home." She smiled. "So where are you planning to take me?"

Vincent laughed. "Tanner filled you in on my intentions, I take it?"

"Generally. Where are you taking me? I'm not exactly dressed for an evening out in this blouse and Dockers."

"You'd look good in a gunnysack, Katie. We're going to the Boulders Resort at Carefree."

"No, not the Boulders!" she protested. "Not with me looking like this!"

* * *

The officer's mouth dropped as he spotted Tanner leaning against the outside of the car. "What the . . ." he gasped. "How did you . . . ?"

"The 'how' doesn't matter," Tanner explained. "What does matter is that we get this little mistake of yours swept under the rug before it gets carried away." Tanner handed back the astounded officer's cuffs and wallet. "I see you work for the sheriff's department, Officer Blake. You guys do outstanding work. I assume you're off duty, right? I mean, even Cory wouldn't have the nerve asking an on-duty officer to pull a prank like this."

The officer shook his head. "You're good, Nelson," he said. "I've heard stories, but I never believed them till now." The officer returned his wallet to his pocket and snapped the cuffs back on his belt. "You know Cory will make life unbearable for you if you ever mention this to a living soul."

"Your secret's safe with me on one condition, Officer Blake. I have a pending emergency and I need to get to my apartment at 59th Avenue and Thunderbird the fastest way possible. A sheriff's escort would be real nice."

"Flashing lights and all, I suppose?" the officer guessed.

"I would appreciate it. And it will get you off the hook when revenge time rolls around for this little joke."

The officer laughed. "Sorry, pal, no can do. Like you say, I'm off duty. I've had all the pranks I can handle for one day. See you around." He got in his car and reached for the ignition key, then stopped, drew a breath, and looked back at Tanner. "My keys?" he asked.

"An escort home?" Tanner countered. "I'll even throw in your service revolver," he said, handing the officer back his own gun.

"You *are* good, Tanner. Give me the keys."

Tanner made it home in just under twenty minutes.

CHAPTER 12

There was no talking Vincent out of the Boulders, so Katherine figured she would just have to grin and bear this one. She wouldn't feel comfortable at this haven for the rich and famous under the best of circumstances, but dressed like this? She wanted to find a hole to crawl into.

According to her watch, it was just after five when the chopper touched down on a section of lawn that doubled as a landing pad. Vincent had the craft secured in a matter of minutes, and then the two of them were on their way to the dining room in a personalized shuttle sent out just for their benefit.

"I've already taken the privilege of ordering," Vincent explained as they approached their table. "The prime rib here is out of this world."

It was obvious to Katherine that Vincent hadn't changed one bit. He was still the same take-charge-of-everything guy she had known and loved throughout their college years. She glanced around, expecting every eye in the room to be on her. No one seemed to be paying the slightest attention. She reasoned this was because Vincent was well-known here and the other diners were being kind out of respect for him.

"So, fill me in," Vincent prompted even before settling in his chair. "What's been going on since you ran off to the Land Down Under?"

"I'm not telling you one thing until you assure me Tanner won't be spending the night in jail."

"He even had that figured out, eh?" Vincent laughed. "Jail wouldn't hurt him. Tanner should know better than to keep you to himself. How come you told him you were coming home and not me?"

"I didn't tell anyone I was coming home," she replied. "Tanner and I met at the airport completely by accident. Tanner was flying in from England, and his flight happened to arrive at the same time as mine."

This brought a laugh. "Can you believe the luck of that guy?" Vincent leaned across the table and patted Katherine's hand. "Enough about Tanner. Are you really home for good, or will you be returning to Australia?"

"My folks live in Australia, Vincent. Naturally I plan to visit them now and then, but as for me ever living there again, I don't think so." Even though Katherine was worried about Tanner, she knew pleading his case with Vincent would only fall on deaf ears. Unless, of course, she told Vincent the reason Tanner needed to get home to his lab. Tanner hadn't said anything about her *not* telling him, but since Vincent's father was so heavily involved, she reasoned otherwise. Why not leave the disclosing to Tanner? Katherine finally concluded that Tanner would find a way to keep the evidence safe, and worst-case scenario would put him at the lab by early morning.

"What were you and Tanner doing in Flag?" Vincent asked, pulling her from her thoughts.

"We went there on a whim," she explained. "We toured the old campus, then took a run by your father's cabin."

"You were at my father's cabin? Why?"

Katherine could kick herself for opening this door. Why had she mentioned the cabin? It had slipped out without her even thinking. "Just for old times' sake," she responded. "The party at your father's cabin is one of my last stateside memories."

Vincent wet his lips. "I'm surprised you got past security. My father has a high-security conference with a bunch of military brass scheduled at the cabin this evening, and he sent two of our most capable men up to secure the place." Vincent hesitated in a moment of thought. "You actually got to the cabin unopposed?" he asked with visible surprise.

Katherine wasn't exactly sure how to answer. While they hadn't been stopped in getting to the cabin, it was after they were there that the trouble set in. She kept her answer simple. "We weren't there very long, Vincent. Even if your men noticed, they didn't confront us."

Vincent was clearly bothered by the apparent lack of security, but to Katherine's relief, he didn't pursue the issue any further. She figured he'd be in touch with his men about it, and she knew those men would report whatever suspicions they had about intruders inside the cabin. She hoped Tanner had covered their tracks well enough, but she wasn't sure. Even though she didn't want to share all she knew with Vincent just yet, she did want to hear what he thought about Brandon's murder. Not that she suspected Vincent could be involved in any way, but still— the evidence *was* found in his father's cabin. She'd have to tread carefully with her questioning. "Let's talk about Brandon," she proposed. "I've only heard bits and pieces of what happened that night."

Vincent exhaled. "None of us really know much about that night," he explained. "We're all certain Troy had nothing to do with it, but . . ." Vincent swallowed. "I consider not being able to help Troy the greatest failure of my life. I exhausted every resource in my power, but whoever framed him did it so well they didn't leave one trace of evidence behind. It's been eight years, Katie. I'm not saying I'm ready to give up, but I am saying the chances of Troy ever being a free man again are rapidly fading."

Vincent's remark about no evidence put Katherine in a tempting position, but she had already decided to not disclose anything without Tanner's approval, and she resolved to stick to that decision. Her next question was one she felt might be better left unsaid, but she risked it. "What about your father's cabin, Vincent? Was it ever checked for signs of foul play?"

Vincent spent the next few seconds apparently fixing an answer in his mind. "You're walking on thin ice, Katie," he finally said. "Thanks to my holding a graduation party at the cabin the same night Brandon disappeared, my father was faced with the monumental task of protecting the name of Wagner Aerospace. At no small expense, my father hired a crew of investigators to go over every inch of the cabin. He oversaw the investigation personally and issued a detailed public report of their conclusions. To answer your question, there were no signs of foul play. Whatever happened to Brandon didn't happen at my father's cabin."

Katherine didn't doubt she had struck a nerve, but she wasn't ready to back off—not with what she knew hanging in the balance.

"Were there other investigators at the cabin besides the ones your father hired?"

Vincent's face had formed into a deep frown by this time. "You have no idea how much pressure came from the press," he informed her. "They all wanted inside the cabin with their television cameras. Fortunately, my father was able to legally block their efforts. He had hired the best, and they pronounced the place clean. What the press wanted was nothing more than journalistic sensationalism."

Hearing this was very upsetting for Katherine. She couldn't be sure whether Vincent was trying to protect his father's name, or if he was, heaven forbid, a part of whatever happened in that cabin that night. "When did Brandon leave the party, and who was he with?" she pressed.

"That is a bit of a strange one," Vincent admitted. "Brandon was supposed to ride home with me, but he slipped out without a word and caught a taxi. I've never been able to figure out that part."

"Did you see Brandon catch a taxi?" Katherine pressed, realizing there had to be something wrong with this assumption in light of what she knew.

"I didn't actually see him," Vincent admitted. "Two of my father's men, Conrad Donahue and Franco Nailor, witnessed it. Even today, Conrad and Franco are two of the firm's most trusted employees."

The conversation was interrupted when the waiter stepped up with soft drinks and bread sticks. Katherine retreated to her own thoughts and felt a chill at the prospect Vincent might be more involved in Brandon's fate than she wanted him to be. By now, she was positive Zachary played a major part in it. Regardless of what her head told her, in her heart she still gave Vincent the benefit of doubt. He was probably taking up for his father out of love and respect. Katherine decided it was time to let this part of the conversation go. Tanner had told her to relax and have a good time, and that's just what she was going to do.

"I think this has gone far enough, Katie," Vincent told her. "And you can put your mind at ease about Tanner; he's not in jail. Cory couldn't talk the officer into that part. Tanner should be on his way home—safe, secure, and pretty darn lonesome."

* * *

Tanner pulled into his apartment lot as the patrol car drove away. "Thanks for the escort," Tanner said under his breath. "It was loads of fun." All the way to his apartment, thoughts of Katherine had filled his mind. Much as he disliked having his time with her cut off so abruptly, he had to admit she deserved to spend some time with Vincent. Tanner would've like to have been able to think of himself as the real reason she came home, but that was pure foolishness. Whatever chance he had with Katherine vanished eight years ago on the front porch of her parents' home.

Stepping through the door, he flipped on the light. Katherine's evening with Vincent would have to be whatever it was. Tanner had work to do, and he wasted no time getting started. Moving to his computer, he turned it on. Three major challenges faced him: matching any fingerprints on the computer disk to Brandon, matching the blood samples to Brandon, and learning what information was recorded on the disk. He started with the disk, where he discovered two distinguishable prints—a thumb and forefinger. It was simple to retrieve a sample of Brandon's prints from his archives, and even simpler to bring up comparable images on his computer screen. "Bingo!" he cried. "We have a match! You did find something on Wagner's computer, didn't you, old friend?"

* * *

"Yes, that's exactly what I did!" came an excited, but unheard voice from one of two angels looking over Tanner's shoulder. "Just keep on trucking, old friend. You're on the road leading straight to my killer."

* * *

Tanner felt a chill that made him stop and glance around the room to be sure he was alone. Crazy as it sounded, he could almost swear he had heard Brandon's voice encouraging him on in his efforts.

Shrugging it off, he moved on to his next item of priority—matching the blood samples.

CHAPTER 13

"We could be on a roll!" Brandon sighed. "Tanner is so close to finding what he needs to bring my case to a close and get Troy out of that stinking prison. But I'm afraid I've gone and blown it, Mitzi."

"What are you talking about?" she asked.

Brandon gazed at her smiling face, where he noticed something he hadn't before. It was her eyes. They were the softest, bluest, most beautiful eyes he had ever seen. How could he have missed noticing them before? He found himself unable to look away, and even more startling was what he was feeling inside. He suddenly wanted this assignment to slow down—perhaps take just a bit longer than it looked like it would. Not that he didn't want things set straight for Troy's sake, but prospects of ending his time with Mitzi so soon were suddenly painful. There was something about her, even more than those fantastic eyes, that Brandon liked. And even the word *liked* didn't seem to be strong enough.

Maybe it was her skill at communicating with people like Katherine and Tanner. She did it with such a soft voice, never raised much above a whisper. Or maybe it was her bubbly personality and constant upbeat attitude that made it almost impossible to keep from smiling in her presence. He didn't know. At the moment, he felt so good he didn't even care about the whys. He would have felt better still if it weren't for one aggravating problem staring him in the face, a problem of his own doing. "My computer disk is password protected," he told her.

"So what's the problem?" Mitzi asked. "Tell me your password, and I'll find a way to get Tanner to think of it."

Brandon rubbed his chin. "That's just it, Mitzi. I can't remember the password. I was under some pretty heavy stress when I copied that disk. Tanner's good at what he does, but the intricacies of computer science is another field altogether. I'm the one who could break through passwords, not Tanner. Without that password, he'll never find what I copied on that disk."

"You forgot the password," Mitzi laughed. "You of all people shouldn't see that as a problem. All you need to do is open a hologram of yourself putting it in the computer. How hard can that be?"

Brandon felt suddenly very foolish. "A hologram?" he muttered. "Why didn't I think of that?" He just overlooked the obvious, that's all. It could happen to anyone.

* * *

Following dinner, Vincent arranged for a chopper ride to get a bird's-eye view of Flagstaff at night. Though he never mentioned it, Katherine assumed he was trying to outdo Tanner's taking her there in his Stingray. Vincent even made one pass over his father's cabin, where the cars and lighted windows gave evidence to the meeting taking place there. The experience wasn't enough to make Katherine forget her concerns over Tanner, nor her fears about Vincent, but it was a breathtaking ride, one she wished didn't have to end so soon. They were almost back to the airport, where the chopper was kept hangared, when Vincent asked a question that she knew he would before the evening ended. "So, where are you staying, Katie?"

This brought a smile, as she knew the reaction she'd get once he was told. "I'm staying in Tanner's apartment," she said with no further immediate explanation. She had to bite her lip to keep a straight face when she saw the look in his eyes. "Tanner moved out," she laughed when she could stand it no longer. "He's bunking down in his lab for the time being."

"That will never do!" Vincent stated abruptly. "You're not even going there tonight! I'll get on the phone and have my secretary find you something more suitable immediately!"

Katherine laughed all the harder. She had hoped for a reaction, but this was more than she had counted on. "Don't bother, Vincent," she told him. "I like my present accommodations just fine." There were multiple reasons behind her decision to stay where she was. No way would she allow Vincent to pay the outrageous price she knew he'd insist on for a place he felt was suitable. Nor was she about to let Vincent or anyone else pick out her permanent living quarters. That privilege was hers alone. She refused to be rushed into finding a place. There was one final reason, and this one more personal. This reason didn't amount to simply Tanner's apartment; it amounted to Tanner himself. She thought she had lost him forever, and now that she had found him again, she just wanted to remain as close to him as possible. If that meant living in a next-door apartment, then so be it. And happily so.

"I'm not taking 'no' for an answer," Vincent insisted. "You're a lady in need of a knight on a white horse, and I'm available. I'll find you a place to stay this very night!"

"And a very handsome knight you make indeed," she observed. "But I really prefer finding my own apartment, Vincent. End of discussion."

"Darn you, Katie Dalton!" Vincent grumbled. "Still playing hard to get! When are you ever going to give up and admit I'm the best thing that could happen to you?"

Again this brought a laugh. "I'm flattered, Vincent, believe me. But choosing between you and Tanner is just too hard a decision right now."

* * *

"Mudbath?" Mitzi asked in shock. "Where did you come up with a password like *mudbath?"*

Brandon closed down the hologram he had used to retrieve the forgotten password. "I remember it now," he sheepishly explained. "When I went looking for a password, I had mudbath on my mind. Vincent had spilled punch on my shirt, remember? Well, what I had in mind for him had something to do with the muddy pond in front of my apartment. He was supposed to take me home that night. I think you can figure out the rest on your own."

"You were facing death and all you could think of was getting back at Vincent? That beats anything I've ever heard."

"I wasn't facing death when I came up with the password, Mitzi. I was about to rejoin the others at the party. It was later, when I went back to the office a second time to make the call to Tanner, that my killers showed up."

"Well, this does present a bit of a problem," Mitzi observed. "When Tanner gets to the point of looking for the password, he'll be thinking of words you might have come up with. But *mudbath?* That's going to be a tough one to reach him with. Why couldn't you have used something like *Katherine?* That would have been obvious."

CHAPTER 14

It was close to midnight by the time Tanner matched the blood samples taken from the cabin to Brandon's. Now he had a string of irrefutable evidence showing Brandon had sustained a disabling wound inside Zachary Wagner's office, probably from a gunshot. The full story of what happened to Brandon was far from complete, but this was a major breakthrough. The next item on the agenda was the information contained on the computer disk. Tanner was positive it was Brandon's stumbling onto that information that got him killed, and he was just as positive that revealing the contents of the disk now would shed some powerful light on the dark secrets surrounding Brandon's demise.

Slipping the disk into his computer and punching in a few commands quickly revealed what he had assumed all along: Brandon had safeguarded the disk with a password. "Okay," Tanner told himself. "We need a password. What would Brandon have used?"

* * *

When Tanner typed in the word *Katherine,* it brought an instant smile to Mitzi's face. She didn't have to say one word to Brandon. The way he refused to look at her was proof enough he knew exactly what she was thinking.

* * *

"So much for the obvious," Tanner said when the file refused to open. "What could Brandon have used? There was a party going on downstairs. I wonder . . ." He typed in one word after another with this thought in mind. *Music, dancing, band, graduation, cap-and-gown* . . . Nothing worked. Next he tried his own name, followed by *Vincent, Troy,* and *Cory.* Another dead end. "Use your head," Tanner groaned in disgust. "What would Brandon have been thinking about?"

* * *

"Mudbath," Mitzi whispered in his ear. "Type in the word *mudbath.*"

* * *

"Blast you, Tanner Nelson!" Tanner chided himself. "This is no time to let nonsense words fill your mind. Think serious!"

It was pathetic. Tanner couldn't shake the one stupid word that kept repeating itself over and over in his mind. Pushing back his chair, he stood, walked to the refrigerator, and poured himself a cold drink of milk. He downed it, then closed the door to his office and remained staring at his computer for several seconds. Still that ridiculous word plagued him. There seemed only one way to get rid of it. Moving back to his keyboard, he typed in the letters one at a time. Eyes widening, he watched the screen light up, revealing an unlocked document. "This is ridiculous," he told himself. "Brandon's ghost can't be here talking with me. But how else could I have come up with a password like *mudbath?* That's not even a real word."

* * *

"The document!" Brandon shouted. "Read the document! Never mind how you got the password. He's not listening to me, Mitzi. You tell him to read the darn thing!"

Mitzi smiled and leaned in close to Tanner's ear. "Read the document," she whispered. "It's what Brandon wants."

* * *

Setting thoughts of ghosts aside, Tanner focused in on the document. He hadn't read a page when a wave of nausea washed over him. No wonder Brandon was so desperate for help in dealing with this. Tanner shot to his feet and slammed an open palm against his chair hard enough to send it tumbling to the floor. "If I'd only stayed at that party another ten minutes, I'd have been there when he needed me," Tanner agonized.

Leaning down, he continued reading until he had finished the entire document. "There's enough evidence here to put you away for the rest of your natural life, Zachary Wagner," he said, the words rolling angrily over curled lips. "Even if I can't get you for Brandon's murder, I've got you for the very reason he was murdered."

Tanner rubbed a hand nervously across his mouth as he considered what else this evidence might indicate. Could Vincent possibly be part of it? The thought made him ill. It would almost be worse than losing Brandon to the hideous crime in the first place. Vincent had to be innocent! Anything else was unthinkable. But even if he was innocent, there was no way to protect him from the fallout disclosing this information was destined to bring. Zachary Wagner was his father. How would Vincent react to Tanner, his own friend, using what he had in his hand to bring Zachary down?

The sound of someone trying to pry the door suddenly pulled Tanner's attention away from the computer. Instantly, his instincts kicked in. It could be nothing or it could be Zachary Wagner's men there to finish the job they started the night of Brandon's murder. Tanner moved quickly, knowing exactly what had to be done before the lock on the door could be defeated. Never was he more glad for his high-speed computer, as well as his trained ear, which had little trouble detecting the sound of a lock pick rolling over the tumblers. He knew he had only seconds remaining. Punching in one final command, he yanked the disk out of the computer and dropped it between the back of the table and the wall. He grabbed the power cord for the computer and ripped it out of the receptacle, causing the screen to immediately go dark. The door then burst open, revealing a man in a black suit sporting a very large handgun with a silencer on the barrel.

Tanner dove for cover behind the edge of the table just as a muffled pop from the man's gun sounded. A stinging sensation in his arm told Tanner he was hit, but not with a bullet. He glanced to see a tranquilizer dart buried deep in his skin. Not good. He realized he had very little time before slipping into unconsciousness, so he had to act fast, and he had to act smart. The sound of footsteps told him the man was closing in. Pulling the dart from his arm, he waited until the assailant was just at the edge of the table. Then, springing to his feet, he planted a hard fist against the man's unsuspecting face, driving him backwards, where he tripped over the fallen chair. Tanner rushed forward, jamming the dart into the back of the man's neck. He realized the amount of tranquilizer left wouldn't put the fellow out, but he hoped it might be enough to slow him down a bit.

Tanner's mind was already numbing. Escape wasn't an option at this point, but there were others. Bursting through the door into the part of the lab he now used as a bedroom, he slammed it closed behind him and snapped the lock. Hurriedly, he moved to the closet and grabbed a pair of shoes and a leather belt. Fighting to remain alert, he replaced the shoes and belt for the ones he had been wearing. He quickly shoved the old ones under the bed and out of sight. The last thing he heard before succumbing to total blackness was the bedroom door being kicked open.

* * *

It was a furious Conrad Donahue who moved to Tanner's limp body and gave it a kick to ensure he was out. "I owe you big-time," Conrad spat out, trying to shake the cobwebs from his head. "No one turns my own weapon on me and gets away with it."

It had taken only a short time for Wagner to run a check on the license plate for the sports car Franco had spotted and to confirm its owner as Tanner Nelson. Conrad and Franco were released of their security roles at the cabin and given the job of dealing with Tanner. By late afternoon, Conrad knew more about Tanner Nelson than he assumed Tanner knew about himself. This was thanks mainly to the avenues available to Wagner Aerospace, avenues not open to just anyone. Neither Zachary nor Conrad had any way of knowing why Tanner was in the cabin, but they were aware he had been close to Brandon Cheney, whom they long suspected had found something about the company that would best be kept buried. The only safe solution to Tanner's sudden interest in Zachary's affairs was to silence him once and for all—exactly as they had Brandon.

Conrad had been lucky in finding Tanner the first place he looked. He knew Tanner held a lease on twin apartments, and since one of those apartments was lit and one was dark, it became obvious which one to check out. Conrad hadn't known for sure Tanner was inside until he opened the door. Seeing Tanner, he had instantly fired the dart. In retrospect, he realized he should have waited long enough for the tranquilizer to take effect before moving in. Tanner was a tough one all right, but not tough enough to deal with Conrad Donahue.

Holstering his gun, Conrad stepped to the window, where he pulled up the shade and peered outside at the parking lot. Franco had already taken care of extinguishing the overhead lights and had pulled the Cadillac around to a point just feet from the apartment window.

Conrad slid the window open just as Franco stepped up to it from the outside. No words were exchanged between the men, since both knew exactly what had to be done. Taking a couple of deep breaths to clear his mind from the effects of the drug, Conrad moved back to where Tanner lay. He emptied Tanner's pockets, placing everything inside a plastic bag to be disposed of later. Everything, that is, except for a ring of keys. Conrad had other uses for these keys, or at least one key he made certain was on the ring. This was the key to a Leer Jet belonging to Tanner's law firm, a jet that remained at Tanner's constant disposal. Conrad had seen the plane many times, as it was kept hangared at Falcon Field Airport, the same airport where Zachary kept his fleet of planes and choppers hangared. Conrad had a special reason for wanting the key—it would make commandeering the Leer Jet that much easier.

Conrad dragged Tanner to the window, hoisted him up, and pushed him through to Franco on the outside. Franco dragged him the rest of the way to the Cadillac and shoved him inside the trunk.

Conrad closed the window and walked back to the main lab, where he examined the computer he had seen Tanner standing in front of when he first entered the room. Glancing at the floor, he discovered the power cord had been unplugged. "Someone wanted to shut this computer down in a hurry, didn't they?" he reasoned aloud. "What do you suppose might be on the files inside it?" Removing all the cords, Conrad lifted the PC, which was no easy task in his half-drugged state. Somehow he made it out of the building, where he joined Franco.

* * *

"It's not fair!" Brandon shouted. "Everything was going perfect, Mitzi! Then these guys show up!" Brandon kicked at the floor before revealing his next bit of information. "These are the same two guys who accosted me in Zachary Wagner's office."

"What?" Mitzi gasped. "These are the men who murdered you?"

"They are, and now they have Tanner in their net. A fine mess I've made of this assignment. I've solved nothing, and now I'm about to get Tanner killed."

Mitzi placed a hand on Brandon's arm. "The authorities didn't send you on this assignment to have it end in failure, Brandon. They know what they're doing."

"I know they know what they're doing. It's me I'm worried about. Have I dropped the ball, Mitzi?"

"I don't have all the answers," she comforted. "But one little setback doesn't spell defeat. Tanner may be facing a problem, but I've seen him come through problems lots of times. And don't forget, he has two highly talented angels looking out for him."

Brandon blew out a long breath as he watched the Cadillac pull out of the lot and make a right turn. "You really think he'll be okay, Mitzi?" he asked.

"I really think so," she assured him. "Now come on. We've got work to do."

* * *

Conrad leaned back in his seat and pondered his next move as Franco pulled the Cadillac onto I-17 and headed for the airport. He hadn't shared the complete plan with Franco just yet—at least not the part about using the jet. But the jet was a perfect piece to the puzzle they were creating to hide the pending fate of Tanner Nelson. Franco would fly the unconscious Tanner to the island using the chopper exactly as planned, but Conrad wouldn't be along for that ride. He'd slip unnoticed into the hangar where the Leer Jet was kept and get it in the air under the guise of Tanner being at the controls. He'd fly it over the island, where he'd radio in a distress call saying he had engine trouble. Then he'd put the craft on autopilot headed out to sea and bail out over the island, where he would rejoin Franco in the chopper. The jet would run out of fuel and crash where it would never be found. The world would think Tanner was in the crash and had simply become shark food. It would be a nice touch to an already-ingenious plan that had once worked with great success in the case of Brandon Cheney.

Franco spoke, interrupting Conrad's thoughts. "What about the woman who was with Tanner at the cabin? What's Zachary's plan for her?"

This was a question that had crossed Conrad's mind as well. "I don't really know what's in the old man's mind," Conrad responded. "But he doesn't want the woman touched. He calls her nothing but a pawn."

Franco's eyes narrowed. "I don't like it," he growled. "Leaving loose ends is sloppy business."

"I don't like it either, Franco, but the man who pays the bills wants it that way."

CHAPTER 15

Vincent was proud of himself for the clever way he had nabbed Katherine from the clutches of his old rival tonight—and what a night it had turned out to be. It was wonderful having her home again. What was it about Katherine that set her apart from other women Vincent had known? She was beautiful, she was so much fun being with, she was a woman who always seemed in control of herself, so in control of any situation she found herself in . . . She was just Katherine, and being just Katherine was what Vincent loved about her and had loved about her since the very first day he ever laid eyes on her. He would gladly have given away every dime of his fortune to hear her say she loved him in return. But try as he might, he could never quite get her to care for him with the same depth he cared for her.

Vincent wasn't blind enough not to know that Katherine's heart leaned toward Tanner. But he didn't care. Deep down he knew, he just knew, it was he who could make Katherine happy—not Tanner. He had reasoned the game was over when Katherine moved to Australia, and he figured both he and Tanner had lost her love. At times he was tempted to pursue his interest in her, even though she had gone away. It would have been so easy for him to go to Australia. But he couldn't bring himself to do that. For as much as he loved her, he still put her happiness ahead of his own. If she had written even once, he would have been on her doorstep in a heartbeat. But she didn't write, and he took that to mean she wanted to take her life in a new direction. So he respected her wishes and didn't go to Australia. He was certain Tanner had reached the same conclusion, and it seemed they had become two casualties of love.

But when Vincent learned Katherine had come home and then that Tanner was already acing him out, the war was on again. He figured eight years was a long time—long enough to change people. Maybe Katherine had changed enough for Vincent to stand a chance at besting Tanner this time around. He wasn't sure about that, but he was sure this had been a perfectly wonderful evening. He was sorry it was almost over. Pulling his Lexus into the apartment complex, he was concerned to see how dark it was. He already hated the idea of Katherine staying here in one of Tanner's apartments, but seeing this only heightened his concern. "Why is this lot so dark?" he asked.

"I don't know," Katherine responded. "It wasn't this way last night."

"Well, it's dark tonight," Vincent grumbled. "Doesn't say much for the maintenance around here. All the more reason to get you into another place, Katie."

* * *

Vincent wasn't the only one wondering about the darkness. For some reason, the overhead light in the parking garage was out. Katherine was glad for her escort, since walking to the building alone was a somewhat frightening thought. Vincent got the door for her, and they stepped inside. "At least the lights in here work," he said. "But I'm seeing you to the door anyway."

Her apartment was at the end of the hall, and reaching it meant going past the one Tanner was now using. As they drew near, she looked to see a sliver of light beneath his door. "Looks like Tanner made it home okay," she remarked.

Vincent rolled his eyes. "Much as I hate the thought, I guess we should check on him."

"You're going to have to face him sometime," Katherine teased. "It might as well be now."

Vincent gave a couple of taps on the door. "My offer still stands for finding you a respectable place to stay," he said as they waited. "If you want to pick out a place yourself, my Lexus is available all day tomorrow, as am I."

"We've already covered this, Vincent. Knock again. I don't think he heard you."

Vincent knocked louder, but there was still no response. "The guy must be asleep," Vincent remarked.

* * *

"Don't leave without checking Tanner's room," Mitzi urged Katherine. "And prepare yourself for a shock, lady. Things haven't gone very smoothly here this evening."

* * *

"Wait!" Katherine said digging through her purse for a set of keys. "Tanner had both of his apartments keyed the same. My key fits his door. I want to check on him." She handed the key to Vincent. "I can't go barging into a man's apartment, but you can."

"Whatever," Vincent said, taking the key and unlocking the door. "But if I wake him, I hope he's not sleeping with a gun." He pushed the door open and glanced around. "Just an empty lab," he said, moving aside for Katherine to look.

At first everything seemed normal, until she looked where Tanner's computer had been. Rushing inside the room, she checked the loose cables. "What is it?" Vincent asked, following her.

"Tanner's computer! It's been stolen! Something's terribly wrong, I know it!"

Vincent's interest suddenly took an upswing. "The door to the bedroom," he exclaimed. "It looks like it's been forced open. This has all the marks of a burglary. But just to be sure . . ." Vincent removed his cell phone from his pocket and punched in a number.

"Who are you calling?" Katherine asked.

"I'm calling Cory. I want to know if he's heard from the officer he talked into pulling the gag on Tanner."

"Yeah, Vince, this is Cory," came the immediate answer. "How'd it go, big man?"

"We may have a problem. I'm in Tanner's apartment, and it looks like a burglar hit him. Did you hear from your friend Officer Blake?"

"Yeah, Tanner turned the tables on him. Blake ended up giving Tanner an escort home."

"Well, he's not here now. Call you back, Cory."

Katherine knew she had to say something now. "There's something I haven't told you, Vincent. Tanner and I did more than just look at the outside of your father's cabin."

Vincent looked puzzled. "You were inside the place? Why, Katie?"

"It's a long story, and one I don't think you're going to like." Katherine was struggling for a way to break the news, and saying she and Tanner were acting on a tip from Brandon's ghost didn't seem appropriate, so she modified the facts some. "Tanner had received an anonymous tip about Brandon's murder," she said. "A tip that led him to your father's upstairs office at the cabin."

A fiery look instantly filled Vincent's eyes. "Someone told Tanner that Brandon was murdered in my father's office? That's an outrageous accusation! I can't believe Tanner would put stock in such a thing! I can't believe it of you either, Katie!"

Katherine took both of Vincent's hands in her own. "We found traces of blood there," she said. "In a pattern Tanner said indicates a shooting."

"NO!" Vincent shouted. "If Tanner found blood, it was from something else! Brandon was *not* murdered in my father's office!"

"There's more," Katherine said, trying to keep her voice calm. "Tanner found a computer disk hidden between the logs right where the blood indicated the shooting victim had fallen."

"So what? My father constantly uses a computer in his office. Why couldn't a disk somehow have gotten where you say Tanner found one? I want this stopped now, Katie! I've got to find Tanner. What you're believing is all a bunch of lies aimed at discrediting my father!"

"I know you're upset, Vincent. I know how much you love your father, and I'm not saying your father is guilty of anything. What I am saying is the evidence points to someone shooting Brandon in that office. We don't know who, and that's why Tanner was bringing the evidence to his lab where he could run tests."

"What kind of tests?"

"Well, for one thing, he wanted to prove one way or the other if the blood he found was Brandon's. He wanted to check for fingerprints on the disk and learn what information was on it. We were trying to get here to his lab when your officer pulled Tanner over."

Katherine paused for a breath, then went on. "You were right about your security men being on the job. They did detect us, Vincent. We avoided them by driving straight through the trees. Tanner said you used that way once to escape some girl's boyfriend."

Vincent's face burned with anger. "You had no right snooping around my father's cabin! I can't explain the things you claim you found, but there's definitely something more going on than what he's concluded. Tanner is my best friend, but this time he's gone too far!"

* * *

"Check the floor behind this table!" Mitzi whispered to Katherine. "If you look close, you can just make out the corner of a computer disk. The disc is important, Katie."

* * *

Katherine lowered her eyes to the point where the table met the wall. "What's this?" she asked, seeing the corner of something that looked like a computer disk. She leaned down and retrieved it. "This is the same disk Tanner found at the cabin!" she exclaimed excitedly.

"Let me see that," Vincent said, yanking the disk from her hand. "Tanner kept a second computer in his other apartment. Is it still there?"

"Yes, it's there."

"Let's go have a look at this."

They moved quickly over to her apartment, where Vincent turned on the computer and inserted the disk. "Blast it!" he shouted, staring at the screen. "The disk is password protected." Vincent removed the disk and shoved it in his pocket.

Katherine started to say something, but Vincent cut her off. "I refuse to leave you here, Katie. Grab whatever you need while I call Cory's sister, Alexis. You can stay at her place for tonight at least."

Katherine considered his suggestion. "You're sure Alexis won't mind?" she asked.

"I'm positive. Alexis loves you, Katie. She'd never stand for me leaving you here under these circumstances." Vincent used his cell phone to make the call.

CHAPTER 16

The first thing Tanner became aware of was the thumping noise of helicopter blades. He struggled to reason through the mental fog clouding his thoughts. The lab . . . A tranquilizer dart . . . He had punched out the intruder, jabbed him with his own dart, and locked himself inside the bedroom . . .

Tanner raised his head to find he was in the backseat of a chopper. There wasn't much light, but enough for him to determine that he and the pilot were the only two on board. He strained to see the pilot. This wasn't the man who broke into Tanner's apartment. This man was balding, and what little hair he did have was mostly gray. The man at the apartment had a full head of black, curly hair.

Tanner suddenly remembered his shoes, drawing a breath of relief that they had gone undetected. He tried to feel for them, only to discover his hands and feet were bound with duct tape. His hands were behind his back, so he reasoned if he could bend his knees just so, he might get a hand on one heel. It was a struggle, but he managed. He glanced out the chopper window and noticed a full moon. He knew it was just about midnight when the intruder entered his apartment. His best guess of the time now would be somewhere around four in the morning.

He blinked, trying to focus his eyes. As he did, he noticed something in the faint light. It was a circular emblem embedded in the leather on the back of the pilot's seat. Tanner knew the emblem belonged to Wagner Aerospace. No big surprise there. But if this fellow at the controls thought he had an easy victim in tow, he was in for one big disappointment.

Bending his knees again, Tanner maneuvered his hand for a solid grip on one heel. Once he had a secure hold, he gave a twist and felt it pull loose from the shoe. His next move would be a tricky one, and he had to be careful not to drop the shoe. He shifted his weight, placing himself in the best possible position. When he was sure he was at just the right angle, he rolled off the seat onto the floor. He had to get the heel jammed under the pilot's seat, where it would remain in place and not be seen. Considering the way they had him hog-tied, this was going to be difficult. Using his knees, he forced himself as close as possible to the back of the pilot's seat. He stretched his arms until the pain in his shoulders told him they were ready to slip from their sockets, then he stretched one more inch. His fingers found a flap in the floor mat that might just do the trick. It took some doing, but he managed to get one edge of the heel under the flap. Then, using his thumb, he continued pushing against it until it was firmly wedged in place.

This done, Tanner turned his attention to the duct tape. If he could find something sharp, he might be able to wear through it. He felt around until his fingers detected a protruding bolt. It wasn't much, but it was all he had. Maneuvering to a point where he could get the greatest leverage, he began a sawing motion. Suddenly he realized the chopper had started a steep descent, indicating they were about to land. He struggled all the harder with the tape, which he had now worn nearly halfway through.

He felt the chopper touch down and heard the engine grind to a stop. The door opened, and he made out the figures of two men, one the pilot and the other the intruder from his apartment. Tanner lay still, faking unconsciousness. He felt the men grab him, yanking him from the chopper onto what felt like the sands of a beach. This was instantly confirmed by the smell of salt and the sound of breaking waves. Wherever they had taken him, it was very near the ocean.

Barely cracking his eyelids, Tanner checked out the men. This second one was definitely the man who accosted him in the apartment, which brought up an interesting point. How had the man gotten there if he wasn't in the chopper?

The pilot spoke. "This guy won't be bothering us much longer, Conrad. Not after we introduce him to the cave that will be his new home."

Cave, Tanner pondered. *What could he mean by that?* He assumed it wouldn't be long before he learned firsthand the answer to that question. At least he had a name for one man now.

"Let's get this over with and get out of here," Conrad responded.

Whatever their intention, they weren't going to be long about it. With one man on each of his arms, they dragged him some distance away from the chopper onto a rocky section of beach. "You watch him," the one called Conrad said. "I'll get the stone."

Again, with slightly parted eyelids, Tanner watched as Conrad moved over to a large, cylindrical-shaped stone. Putting his weight into it, Conrad gradually moved it to one side, revealing what appeared to be the entrance of a cave. Conrad returned, and together the men dragged Tanner over to the cave and shoved him inside. Seconds later, he heard the stone being rolled back into place.

Realizing he was now out of their sight, Tanner sprang into action. He quickly found a sharp rock and finished cutting through the tape on his hands. Next, he freed his feet. It took only a moment to realize there would be no moving the stone from inside—it would be impossible to get enough leverage. This meant the exit was completely blocked.

Tanner felt for his belt. "I see you boys missed this little item, too," he said, twisting the buckle, which slipped off in his hand. Inside the buckle were two items, both of which Tanner needed at the moment. One was a miniature flashlight, the other a device Tanner had in mind for a special use. This one he slipped in his pocket for the time being. The flashlight he snapped on, as the only light inside the cave was the moonlight that weakly filtered in through the cracks of the entrance.

As the beam of Tanner's light pierced the darkness of the cave, he could tell it extended some distance back. He began inching his way back, all the while checking for any possible way out. He had gone about twenty feet when he came to a small opening. It was too small for him to squeeze through but large enough to afford a good view of the outside. What he first saw brought a start. Even at low tide, the waves were only inches below the opening. Reason told him that with the incoming tide, this whole cave would fill with ocean water—not a pretty thought for someone trapped inside.

Moving deeper into the cave, he discovered an upper ledge that seemed to be the highest point. The ledge was easily large enough to accommodate a man, which interested Tanner. If someone were inside this cave when it was filling with water, the ledge might have become a place for a last-ditch effort to remain alive. *I wonder if these culprits have used this cave before? Perhaps for the purpose of an execution chamber?*

Pulling himself up, Tanner shone the light over the surface of the ledge. Something white caught his eye. It was jammed between two rocks, so Tanner stretched out his arm and pulled it loose, examining it under the light. It was a skull. A human skull. "Looks like I was right," he observed. "I'm not the first visitor to this cave. You've been a very bad man, Zachary Wagner. It looks like I'm going to have to bring you down even if you are my best friend's father."

Checking the shelf more closely, Tanner realized there were more bones. Enough, he estimated, to make a complete skeleton. Then he spotted something else. Very carefully, he reached out and picked it up. "Oh, no," he gasped, seeing it was a gold pocket watch. Running his thumb over the raised image of a telescope facing a star-filled sky, Tanner knew what he had found. This was Brandon's watch, the one given to him by his grandfather. Tanner swallowed and let out a muffled moan as he realized he had just uncovered Brandon's tomb.

* * *

"This is how you died?" Mitzi asked, staring at his skull.

"You make it sound more grim than it really was," Brandon quietly explained. "Not that I wasn't scared out of my wits. But you know the story, Mitzi. As the darkness closed in, it was replaced by streamers of brilliant light. And right there in the middle of that light stood a woman with a smile warm enough to conquer all my fears."

"Who was she?" Mitzi asked.

"My grandmother. And what a shock to see her looking younger and more beautiful than I ever remembered her."

"Oh, yes," Mitzi giggled. "How glad I was to learn that 'old' is a stigma attached only to mortality. I never reached that stage in my own mortal life, but I would have hated it, believe me."

"You died young too?" Brandon asked.

"I was thirty. A drunk driver ran a red light. One second I was driving along University Boulevard in Denver, Colorado, and the next I was looking into that same brilliant light. It was my grandfather who picked me up." She laughed. "He was also much younger than I remembered him."

"You died in a car accident? Did it bother you looking at your own body?"

"Of course it bothered me. I looked a mess, and there was nothing I could do about it."

Brandon laughed. "You were worried about what some medic was going to think when he saw the condition of your hair?"

"Yes! It still bothers me, just thinking about it."

"Yeah, well, it sort of bothers me seeing my own skull and bones, but not for the same reason. It's just eerie, that's all. I guess it was lucky I climbed up on that ledge; otherwise Tanner might not have found me. Or—you know—that part of me."

"I know what you meant, Brandon."

"It wasn't easy climbing up there. I had been shot, you know. I was pretty weak."

"Maybe you had some help. Your grandmother might have put in a word with the authorities."

"That's probably right. I'll have to ask her next time I see her."

At that instant, the sound of the helicopter being started broke the stillness. "Oh, no!" Mitzi gasped. "Those guys are getting away! Come on, Brandon, do something!"

"Do what?" Brandon asked. "There's no way he can move that stone by himself, and we certainly can't help him. He's in the same fix I was in, and there was never a time in my whole mortal life when I was so helpless."

"You forget, I'm Tanner's guardian angel. I've seen him in tighter fixes than this. Not only that, I'm sure the authorities would never let things get this far without a way out. They're not going to doom your assignment to failure, Brandon—not because of something you have no control over."

"I wish I were so optimistic, Mitzi. But if I couldn't find a way out, how can he?"

Brandon looked over at Tanner, who had moved back to the opening, giving himself an unobstructed view of the ascending chopper. "Leaving so soon, fellows?" Tanner asked. "The party's just getting started."

Mitzi gave Brandon a gently nudge on the shoulder. "Told you so, didn't I?" she teased. "He has something up his sleeve. Just watch."

Tanner pulled something from his pocket. "What's he got?" Brandon asked.

"I'm not sure yet," Mitzi responded. "Whatever it is, it came from the compartment he had hidden in his belt buckle, the same as the flashlight."

Brandon nodded. "I saw him take something out and stick it in his pocket. I think we're about to find out what it is."

Holding the small device out the opening in the rocks, Tanner aimed it at the chopper. "Say hello to my friend Brandon!" he said, pressing his thumb against a detonator switch. The report from the explosion was deafening. Being an angel, Brandon had no trouble moving outside, where he saw the chopper in a ball of flames and smoke. "Wow!" he said to Mitzi, who was right behind him. "Tanner had a bomb. It must have been inside the heel of his shoe that he planted under the pilot's seat."

"And the object he had hidden in his belt buckle was some kind of remote detonator," Mitzi added.

As the angels watched, the chopper fell in two sections. The front half, where both men had been, crashed into the ocean, disappearing beneath the rolling water. The rear half was thrown back toward land, falling at a point where the beach merged into a section of dense vegetation. "They never knew what hit them," Mitzi observed. "They messed with the wrong guy when they messed with Tanner Nelson."

"Who, by the way, is still trapped inside the cave," Brandon pointed out. The angels checked back inside to find Tanner at the stone blocking the exit. "You can't move it, buddy. It's too heavy," Brandon lamented.

"He's not trying to move it," Mitzi said. "Look, he has another explosive."

As Brandon watched in amazement, Tanner removed the heel from his second shoe and crammed it into a crevice between the stone and the solid rock wall. "He's going to blast his way out!" Brandon exclaimed.

"So it would seem," Mitzi agreed. "How far back does this cave extend?"

"Far enough to keep him safe, just as long as he stays low and behind the cover of the rocks. But the sound of the explosion is going to give him one hummer of a headache."

"I vote we don't hang around in here to verify that, Brandon."

"Good point. Tanner's smart enough to take care of himself. We might as well wait outside."

CHAPTER 17

The two angels emerged from the cave to an unexpected sight as Conrad Donahue stumbled from the water onto the beach. "What happened?" Conrad gasped, holding his head. "The chopper exploded. I don't get it."

"Guess what we're about to witness?" Brandon grinned. "This could be entertaining."

"Could be," Mitzi agreed. "Since Tanner's okay for the moment, what do you say we kick back and watch?"

"Sounds like a plan. Look, Franco is coming up behind his cohort. I think I'm going to enjoy this."

"Look at that thing," Franco said pointing to the section of broken chopper that landed on the beach. "How'd we come out alive?"

"I don't know," Conrad responded. "My cell phone's gone. You still got yours?"

Franco checked. "No, I've lost mine, too. How we gonna get off this rock with no transportation and no communication?"

"Wagner will send someone looking for us. I can't figure out what happened. The chopper seemed fine, then it just blew. I've been flying those things for years and never experienced anything like that."

Brandon and Mitzi watched as the figure of a third man walked up the beach to where they stood. "Morning, Brandon, Mitzi," the fellow said as he approached.

"Morning, Gabe," Brandon returned. "Out for a trash pickup this early, are you?"

"It's a dirty job, but some angel has to do it."

Both Brandon and Mitzi were acquainted with Gabe. They knew he was from the lower-side greeting department, here to escort Conrad and Franco to their new facility. Unlike the sort of greeting Brandon and Mitzi received when they stepped from mortality, Conrad's and Franco's kind rated a different reception. No grand-mother, no grandfather, no special friend, just someone from the lower-side greeting department. "If you two will excuse me a minute," Gabe said, "I'll get this pickup started."

* * *

Neither man had noticed Gabe until he stepped up behind them. "Excuse me, gentlemen, might I have a word with you?"

Both men whirled to see who had spoken. "Who are you?" Conrad demanded, searching frantically for his gun that seemed to be missing.

"Interesting question," Gabe responded. "Who were you expecting exactly, your friendly neighborhood welcome wagon?"

"Your gun!" Conrad barked at Franco. "Give it to me!"

"I don't have it! I must have lost it in the crash!"

Gabe raised a hand, trying to ease the tension. "It's okay, boys. You won't be needing guns where you're going."

"Who are you?!" Conrad demanded a second time.

"Name's Gabe. I'm your transportation off this rock."

Conrad did a double take. "Do you work for Wagner?"

"Oh, no. I report to someone much higher than Zachary Wagner. Now, if you gentlemen are ready, can we get started?"

"I'm not going anywhere!" Conrad snapped. "Not without some answers! Who do you work for, and where is it you want to take us?"

Gabe let out a lingering sigh. "You fellows haven't figured it out yet, have you?"

"Figured what out?" Franco cut in.

Gabe paused a moment, just looking at them. "You were in a helicopter crash, gentlemen. A horrendous one."

"So tell me something I don't know," Conrad rebutted. "We survived a crash, so what? That still doesn't explain this little game of yours."

Gabe motioned for Brandon and Mitzi to join him. Until now they hadn't been noticed. "I'd like you fellows to meet a couple of friends of mine," Gabe said as the two stepped up. "The pretty one is Mitzi Palmer. The other one is someone I suspect you fellows know."

"It can't be!" Franco shrieked, pulling back a step and searching again for his missing gun. "You're dead!"

"No," Conrad said, keeping a much cooler head. "This can't be who you think it is, Franco. He's just a look-alike." Conrad raised a finger, which he waved in Gabe's face. "I want some answers, and I want them now. What are you doing on this island, and what's this thing about you being our transportation out of here?" At that instant, a flash of lightning bolted from the sky, striking at a point between Conrad's feet. Fire and sparks flew as the boom of thunder shook the ground. Conrad screamed and jerked back.

"Sorry about that," Gabe said. "Sometimes I lose it when I get a finger in my face. Nothing I know agitates me quite like that."

Gabe stepped forward and stood looking into the eyes of the shaken man. "Fine morning for a pickup, wouldn't you say? The sun will be breaking through any minute now. Ever seen a sunrise over this island? It can be breathtaking."

Gabe glanced over at Franco, then back at Conrad. "Now let me explain something to you gentlemen as plainly as I know how. You're both dead. As in expired, passed away, deceased. Any way you cut it, the book just closed on your time in this world. So, you see, when I said I'm your transportation off this rock, I didn't mean back to Arizona."

A look of horror filled the face of both men. "I can't be dead!" Conrad exclaimed, patting himself down. "I don't feel any different!"

"You're not supposed to feel different," Gabe explained. "That's the way it works. And by the way, I just finished looking over the pickup papers for the two of you. You should be ashamed. You both did some naughty things in mortality. Pity. But there'll be plenty of time for you to think about that after I drop you off."

"Uh-oh, Mitzi," Brandon spoke up. "Cover your ears. It's about to happen." The explosion caught only Conrad and Franco by surprise. The others were ready for it.

"What was that?" Conrad cried.

Brandon stepped forward. "That was my friend Tanner Nelson making pebbles out of the stone you had covering the cave entrance. You may have sentenced me to an untimely drowning, but you couldn't outdo Tanner."

Conrad slunk back. "It really is you!" he gasped.

"It's him," Mitzi affirmed. "Looks a lot better than the last time you saw him, doesn't he?"

Gabe spoke up again. "I'd like to stay here and chat some more, but I'm on a busy schedule. Come on, gentlemen. It's time. And don't make me use any more lightning bolts. That sort of thing gets a little dramatic."

CHAPTER 18

Stepping through his newly created doorway, Tanner gulped in several breaths of clean air. He glanced up to see the sun just breaking through the morning sky. "Okay," he said. "Now the question is, where exactly am I? It's a deserted beach—that much is obvious. The problem is finding what part of the planet the beach is on." He knew it had to be somewhere fairly remote in order for Brandon's body to have gone unnoticed the past eight years.

Shading his eyes, he checked the position of the sun and suddenly realized that either the sun was rising in the west or the ocean was to his east. He had assumed he was someplace on the Pacific coast, but that theory had just died. How could the sun possibly *rise* over the west coast? "I'm on an island," he reasoned. "There's no other explanation."

He could see that this island—if that's what it was—was made up of a mountain, a beach area, and a densely vegetated rain forest. The mountain was off to his left, where the cave was situated. The beach was to his right, and the rain forest was inland beginning about a hundred feet back from the surf. What he wanted now was to look things over from the highest point. He did a visual check of the small mountain. It appeared climbable, but only with some difficulty since it was a highly rocky terrain. "Might as well get started," he said. "Just looking at it won't get the job done."

The climb didn't prove to be as bad as he had expected. He reached the top in about twenty minutes, and from there he could tell for sure he was on an island, albeit a small one—probably no more than a mile and a half across at the widest point. Just as he expected, there were no signs of habitation.

Tanner moved over and knelt down next to a pool of water. Scooping up a handful, he found it sweet to the taste. "Rain water," he calculated. "From the amount of vegetation here, it's apparent the rainfall has to be heavy." He drank his fill.

Next he moved to a point where the beach below him was visible and noticed the downed section of the chopper, something he had overlooked before. Since it had fallen at a point where the beach and rain forest came together, it was partially obscured by the undergrowth.

Looking farther up the beach, he spotted something else of interest. "A parachute," he mused. "An old military camouflage chute. Haven't seen one of those around in a while." The parachute might explain how Conrad got onto the island without being in the chopper. "But why would he have parachuted here? I must be missing something somewhere."

Satisfied he had seen all he could from this point, Tanner started back down. Once he reached the beach, he headed straight for the wreckage. "It's only the rear section," he noted. "The front must have been ripped off in the explosion. Probably fell in the ocean. I wonder if anything useable might be left in this mess."

He moved closer. "Well, what do we have here?" he said, checking what had been a storage compartment. "A toolbox. That might come in handy." Tanner pulled the box out and placed it next to the trunk of a nearby palm tree. Next he found a fifty-foot length of nylon rope and a half-used roll of duct tape. These he placed next to the toolbox. A continued search turned up something of special interest, a mobile phone built into one of the armrests. The phone itself seemed undamaged, but it lacked one thing. It had received power from the chopper's battery, which had been wiped out in the crash. Without power, the phone was useless. Tanner set it with the other items anyway.

There was still one item he wanted to check out—the black box designed to transmit a locator signal upon impact. In all probability, the black box was transmitting its signal even now, which could be good or bad. There was no doubt the explosion had happened too fast for the chopper pilot to send out a distress call, so the first indication of a problem wouldn't come until the chopper was late returning to base. Even then, no one outside Zachary's organization would know, and those within the company wouldn't want anyone snooping around this island, not with the secret they knew lay hidden here. Even if they did report a chopper down, they certainly wouldn't give any hint it might be in this area. If anyone did come checking, it would be Zachary's men. It therefore became an advantage for Tanner to silence the black box. Why lead the enemy right to his door? Finding the black box and disabling it had a second advantage too. It would mean saving the battery for some future time when a signal might become helpful.

Locating the black box was easy and so was removing it, thanks to the tools he had found. He opened it carefully so as not to disrupt its usability later on and simply disconnected the battery leads to shut it off.

One important job remained. When Zachary's men did come looking for the downed chopper, Tanner wanted them to think it crashed somewhere out in the ocean, not here on the island. He knew the wreckage wasn't all that detectable from land, but it could be spotted without too much problem from the air. What he needed was a way to camouflage the wreckage, and what better way to do it than with an old military camouflage parachute?

CHAPTER 19

Mel Phillips leaned back in his desk chair and glanced through his office window at a hangar filled with aircraft. To Mel, there was nothing more beautiful than discovering freedom beyond each new cloud. Acquiring the job as maintenance director overseeing the fleet of Wagner Aerospace's airborne transportation was a dream come true for Mel. Even now, fifteen years into the job, Mel wouldn't trade places with any man alive. Not that the job didn't have its downside, such as Mel's lack of trust and respect for the company's founder. Mel always suspected that Zachary Wagner conducted his share of shady deals, but Mel figured since he was concerned only with the aircraft, the rest of what the company did was none of his business.

As Mel watched the maintenance crew at work, he noticed a man wearing a dark business suit and carrying a briefcase step inside the hangar. Mel recognized him as Winston Harmon, a top company executive and the man Mel reported to directly. "Good morning," Mel said as Winston stepped into his office. "What can I do for you?"

It was always obvious how out of place Winston felt inside the hangar office. He was most certainly a man accustomed to finer surroundings. Normally all business conducted between these two men was done by phone. "I just got word from The Man that Conrad and Franco might be in trouble," Winston responded. "They took one of the choppers out on an assignment, and they haven't reported in. It's been several hours."

Mel had noticed one of the choppers missing when he showed up for work, but he thought little of it since it was common for the company pilots to take an aircraft out without telling him. "Are you hinting at a possible craft down?" Mel asked.

Winston nodded. "There is some concern. The Man would like it checked out." Hearing Winston refer to Zachary as *The Man* always bugged Mel. There was just something sinister in it. But who was he to argue with Winston?

"Have you reported this to the FAA?" Mel asked.

"No! We have a touchy situation here. The Man wants it handled in-house."

This didn't sound good to Mel, but neither did it surprise him. It was just the way Zachary Wagner worked sometimes. "I know someone took number 7 out, but they didn't bother filling me in on a flight plan," Mel explained. "Which is nothing unusual. It happens all the time. But if I'm to conduct a search, I'll need to know where to start looking."

"They were flying on an assignment over Butterfield Island," Winston responded. "That's all you need to know."

Butterfield Island was a company code name for a small island just off the coast of Mexico where Wagner Aerospace reportedly conducted some highly secretive experiments. The only reason Mel knew of the island came by accident when he happened onto a map showing its location. The map was one Conrad had inadvertently left inside the chopper after returning from a job several years earlier. When Mel mentioned the map and the island to Winston, he was told of its secret nature and sworn to silence on the subject. "I'll need to see the map showing the location of the island," Mel proposed now. "I only saw it once, and that was years ago."

Winston removed a copy of the map from his briefcase and handed it to Mel. "Don't show this to anyone, and I want it back as soon as your search is finished."

"I take it you want me to conduct this search personally?"

"That's the way The Man wants it. And regardless of what you find, you report back to no one but me. Is that understood?"

Mel considered this. "What if I find them in need of help? You know, in a life raft, or . . . ?"

"Regardless of what you may find, you report only to me!" Winston said again. "What we're dealing with here is of the utmost sensitivity."

"All right, Mr. Harmon, I'll do as you say." Mel had learned long ago to play the game with Winston. If he hadn't, he strongly suspected he would have been out of the best job he'd ever stand the chance of holding down.

"Good," Winston stated shortly. "Naturally I want you to check the water between here and the island, but I also want you to check the island itself."

"I'll use one of the choppers," Mel suggested. "That way I can land if I do spot something on the island."

"No, take one of the jets. That'll speed up your search. If a rescue is necessary, we'll handle it when the time comes. And do not—I repeat—do not use the radio to pass along anything you find. If you do run into something of interest, call in with the message, *I'm on my way home with the groceries.* I'll know what you mean, and I'll be waiting here when you land. If you don't spot anything of interest, just hold your silence." Winston closed his briefcase and asked, "Any questions?"

"I think I have it down," Mel answered.

"Good, then get to it. And remember, this is a highly sensitive mission. Don't foul it up."

CHAPTER 20

Katherine watched as Alexis downed her last bite of toast with a drink of milk, rinsed her dish and glass, then slid them in the dishwasher. "Sorry to rush off like this," Alexis apologized. "I should have been at the hospital ten minutes ago. All part of the game in a nurse's life. I never know when they might call me in for emergency coverage."

Katherine was grateful beyond words for Alexis's kindness in allowing her to stay in her home the past night, a sleepless night filled with worry about Tanner. "I understand perfectly," she replied.

Alexis grabbed her purse and headed for the door. "I have no idea how late I'll be, so just make yourself at home. I'm sure Vincent will check on you sometime this morning."

Katherine remained standing at the open door until Alexis's little Volkswagen Cabrio pulled out of the driveway and headed down the street. Returning to the kitchen table, she picked up her half-finished glass of orange juice but didn't take a drink. Katherine hated being alone when something was bothering her. She needed someone to lean on at times like this. Try as she might, she couldn't get thoughts of Tanner out of her mind. It just didn't make sense, his running off the way he did without one word. And leaving that computer disk where he did, between his table and the wall. Why would he do that when the disc was such a strong piece of evidence for solving the mystery of what happened to Brandon? No matter how she looked at it, it just didn't add up.

Katherine glanced up as a knock sounded at the door. She felt strange answering the door in someone else's home, and she wasn't in the mood for long explanations as to why she was here and Alexis wasn't. Still, she couldn't just sit here and ignore whoever it was.

Setting the orange juice down, she moved to the door and opened it. "Vincent?" she gasped at the sight of him. "Thank goodness it's you."

"Bad night?" Vincent guessed after taking a moment to look her over.

"Does it show that much?"

"I'm afraid it does," he admitted.

Katherine couldn't take offense at this. She had curled her hair with a borrowed curling iron that had a barrel three times the size of her own, and all the makeup she had with her was what she carried in her purse. That, added to the bags under her eyes, didn't exactly qualify her for a Miss America contest this morning. But Vincent could have shown a more sensitive side by not mentioning it. "Thanks," she rebuffed. "You really know how to bolster a girl's self-esteem. But you're right, it was a bad night. Any word about Tanner?"

Vincent didn't answer right away. "May I come in?" he asked.

Katherine, sensing something was wrong, moved aside as he came in, then closed the door behind him. "What is it?" she pressed.

Vincent blew out a loud breath. "I have some news, Katie."

Katherine's face felt suddenly hot. "What news?" she asked.

Vincent pulled her to his chest, where he held her for several seconds before going on with his explanation. "I just heard from Cory," he said at last. "There's been a breaking news bulletin. The pilot of a Leer Jet radioed in from a location somewhere off the coast of Mexico. He reported engine trouble just before the transmission went dead."

Katherine stiffened and forced her eyes tightly closed as Vincent went on with some of the hardest news she had ever heard. "The pilot identified himself, Katie. It was Tanner." Tears rolled down her face as Katherine buried her head against Vincent's shoulder. "There's been no sign at all of a wreckage," Vincent continued. "You know Tanner as well as I do. He's probably out there in a rubber life raft catching some rays."

Katherine backed away and brushed a hand over one eye. "Be honest with me, Vincent. What are his chances?"

"Katie, I . . ."

"Just tell me Vincent. I need to know."

"All right," he sighed. "The transmission was too short to pinpoint a location with any accuracy, and he didn't file a flight plan. That places him somewhere in the middle of one huge ocean with no clue where to begin a search."

Katherine buried her face in both hands. This just wasn't fair. A whole new world had opened when Tanner stepped back into her life, and now that world was shattering before her very eyes.

"Where's Cory's sister?" Vincent asked.

"She was called to the hospital on an emergency. Something about a five-car pileup on I-10. You didn't miss her by five minutes."

Vincent placed a hand on Katherine's arm. "I don't want you to be alone, Katie. I had a business flight scheduled to Puerto Rico, but I asked to have someone else sent in my place."

"Thank you," she choked out. "I really don't want to be alone. But I just can't understand. Tanner was onto something he felt was very big. There's no way he would have gone off on some job without a word of explanation. It doesn't add up."

"It does add up, Katie, with Tanner. His job is his life. The distress call proves he was headed somewhere in the company jet."

Katherine wasn't buying it, but she was in no mood to argue. She did have one question that needed to be asked, though. "What did you do with the disk we found in Tanner's lab?"

"I spent a couple of hours last night trying to crack the password. I'm just not that computer savvy. This morning I put the disk in the hands of an expert."

Katherine caught her breath. "You what?! You let that disk out of your hands? How could you, Vincent? That disk may contain information about Brandon's fate."

Vincent shook this off. "I'm positive the disk has nothing to do with Brandon. I have no idea why there would be bloodstains in my father's office, but I know whatever the explanation, it's perfectly innocent. I gave the disk to Cecil Romero, the head of our computer department. If anyone can crack the password, it'll be Cecil."

"You had no right!" Katherine rebuked. "I don't care if you're trying to protect your father; that disk should be placed in the hands of the authorities. If, as you say, it had no incriminating information on it, then it would have gone for naught. I'm begging you, Vincent. Get that disk back now!"

"Katie, the disk is perfectly safe in Cecil's hands. But if it means that much to you, I'll get it back. I'll have him make a copy of it."

"You'll get it back from him when?" Katherine pressured.

"Today. I promise. Have you had breakfast?"

"I had some orange juice. I'm really not in the mood for food."

"You've got to eat, Katie. You won't be any help to Tanner or anyone else if you don't keep up your strength. Grab your purse and come on; we're going to get you some breakfast."

Katherine really wasn't hungry, but she went along with him simply because she didn't want to be alone.

* * *

Tanner moved back a step to evaluate his efforts at camouflaging the chopper. It would do nicely. Only the closest inspection would possibly reveal anything out of the ordinary from the air. He had just finished the job when the sound of a jet abruptly reached his ears. Seconds later the craft came into view. It proved to be a Leer Jet, similar to the one Tanner flew for his company. "That'll be some of Zachary's bunch now," he said, crouching low behind a cluster of palm trees. "I'm surprised it's a jet and not a chopper. No threat of them landing that thing here, but if they learn this is where those two dupes bought the farm, they'll be back."

The jet made a pass over the island so close Tanner could nearly count the rivets on the fuselage. It was one of Wagner's. Tanner remained low, figuring the pilot would make a second pass before heading out, and he was right. This second flyover came from the opposite direction. Tanner now reasoned one of two things would follow. If the pilot had seen anything that caught his attention—anything at all—he'd make another pass. Or, if Tanner's disguise had worked and the pilot had seen nothing, then he'd most likely set a course back for the mainland and continue searching for traces in the water. Tanner held his breath and watched. To his great relief, the plane never turned. It soon became nothing more than a dot against the deep blue sky and then vanished altogether.

* * *

When Mel failed to see any sign of the missing chopper on Butterfield Island, his natural instinct was to notify the FAA of a possible downed craft. If Conrad and Franco had gone down over water, their only real chance for survival would depend on a concentrated effort by the coast guard, who were equipped with all the proper resources. What chance did one man in a company jet have of finding them? Especially considering the miles of ocean that needed to be covered and that the visible signs of where the crash took place might be little more than some floating debris or an oil slick? Mel's resources didn't include high-tech tracking equipment to home in on the locator signal that was probably being transmitted this very minute. Notifying the FAA was the right thing to do, but it would cost Mel his job—this he knew. It was the hardest decision of his life, but in the end he kept the radio silence Winston had ordered and set a course for Falcon Field.

After landing and before securing the aircraft, Mel set out to call Winston on one of the highly secure in-house phones. He knew that using a cell phone would be strictly out of the question. Mel punched in the number for Winston's office and breathed a relieved sigh when Winston picked up. If Winston had been out of his office, all Mel could have done was leave a message, and this was no time for leaving messages, with the lives of two men possibly at stake.

"I combed the area between here and the island," Mel explained. "And I made two low-level passes over the island itself. I don't suppose there's been any word since we spoke?"

"You're saying you found nothing?" Winston barked.

"No, not a trace." Mel didn't ask again about further word coming in about the missing plane; he assumed from Winston's response there hadn't been any. "What else do you want me to do, Mr. Harmon?" Mel considered his next suggestion carefully before voicing it. "Should I contact the FAA yet?"

"Absolutely not! I'll take it from here, Mel. You just forget you ever heard a word about this, understand?"

The line went dead, and Mel dropped his receiver back to the hook. For more than a minute, he stood staring at the phone on his desk, toying with the idea of making that call to the FAA. How could he ever look himself in the mirror again if those men should die because he did nothing? Picking up a picture of his wife and two daughters, he ran a finger over the glass. Thanks to his lucrative job, they lived very comfortably in a beautiful Paradise Valley home, and money for the girls' educations would be there when the time came. He wet his lips, then slowly returned to the hangar to secure the jet.

CHAPTER 21

Anger burned in Winston's mind at thoughts of having to bring a fool like Mel Phillips in on something this serious. Unfortunately, the only pilots Winston could trust were the two missing in the presumed crash, Conrad and Franco. The only choice he had, other than Phillips or one of the regular pilots, would have been flying the reconnaissance mission himself. That was an option he preferred not to consider, as it had been years since he had piloted anything, let alone a chopper. It would require a pretty big emergency for him to take the stick again.

He couldn't help but feel edgy about revealing to Mel the things he had, and he certainly didn't want to let him in on anything more. Winston was aware of Conrad's plan to commandeer Tanner's Leer Jet and send the distress call in Tanner's name. He also knew the distress call had been picked up, and a search for the jet Tanner was supposedly flying was underway. Fortunately, this search was taking place farther out to sea than Butterfield Island, meaning the chances of anyone happening onto the chopper crash were extremely slim.

Winston also knew that if Conrad had successfully made the phony distress call, he had to have been alive when the time came for him to bail out over the island. The logical conclusion was that Conrad and Franco met up on the island, did the job they set out to do, and met with an unseen tragedy on the way back to Falcon Field. They might have crashed on land, but that was less likely than the ocean. A crash on land would come closer to having been reported.

The loss of two men such as Conrad and Franco was certainly a blow to Wagner Aerospace, but in this line of business, there were always risks. The mission they were sent to do was absolutely necessary. Tanner Nelson had to be taken care of. He knew too much, evidenced by what the computer department had found on the hard drive of Tanner's computer. That, as well as the recovered floppy disk. It was really ironic, the way that computer disk found its way home after lying hidden right under their noses all these years. To think Brandon Cheney had managed to hide it completely unobserved. In a way, Tanner's curiosity paid off in big dividends for Wagner. Granted, if Tanner had gotten away with his intentions, Wagner Aerospace would have been in hot water, but thanks to Conrad's quick action, everything was now back in check. Both the disk and the information Tanner had transferred to his lab computer wound up in Cecil Romero's hands and had now been totally obliterated. What Tanner had actually managed to do was eliminate all chance of that disk ever surfacing.

Winston picked up the security phone again. It was time to fill Zachary in on this latest information. Winston had hesitated this long because he knew how Zachary would feel about having to take action against Katherine Dalton. But it was obvious she now knew more about the contents on the disk than Zachary could safely overlook. He'd have to reconsider his opinion of her as being only a pawn. The situation called for dealing with her and doing it swiftly. He punched in Zachary's private number and waited for The Man to pick up.

* * *

"Thanks for breakfast," Katherine told Vincent as they left the restaurant on their way to the parking lot. "I didn't think I was hungry, but those eggs tasted pretty good."

"Like I said, you have to keep up your strength. I was wondering if you'd like to stop by the radio station to see if Cory might have learned anything more?"

"That sounds as good as anything right now. I've never felt more helpless in my life."

Vincent opened the door, and Katherine slid inside. She pulled out a tissue and dabbed her eyes. Just as he closed her door, she felt a painful sting in her left shoulder. Jerking her head around, she was astounded to see a man in a dark suit behind her holding a hypodermic needle he had unmistakably just used to inject her with something. She tried to scream, but no sound came from her throat. Her tongue felt swollen, and her mind whirled dizzily. She glanced at Vincent, but her vision was too blurred to make out his expression. Was he a part of what was happening? Was Tanner really missing in a plane, or was this a trumped-up story used to distract her long enough for her to fall through a trapdoor? One final thought passed through her mind. *Am I about to meet the same fate as Brandon?* Then there was only darkness.

* * *

"Come on, Brandon," Mitzi pleaded as she watched him pace back and forth outside Vincent's Lexus. "Things will work out. Don't give up the ship before the cannons are even loaded."

Brandon threw up both arms. "I made a mistake, Mitzi! I thought if Katherine found the computer disk, it would be a home run for our side. I should never have asked you to whisper the location of the disk to her. Now look what's happened!"

Mitzi placed both hands on her hips. "Where's your faith?" she scolded. "So you didn't get your home run. It's not the ninth inning yet."

"Not the ninth inning? How do you figure? Tanner's wandering around on a rock in the ocean while the whole world thinks he was killed in a plane crash, the evidence I saved on that disk that might have brought Zachary Wagner down has been eradicated, Katherine's life has just fallen squarely into the hands of Wagner Aerospace—what else could you call it but the ninth inning, Mitzi?"

"Okay, so maybe it is the ninth inning, but there are still three outs to go. We're going to win this game, Brandon. I know how the authorities work, and I know they wouldn't have sent you on this assignment unless they were sure you were the right one for the job. Now, get ahold of yourself. We have work to do."

CHAPTER 22

Tanner snapped his fingers as an idea suddenly crossed his mind. Why hadn't he thought of it before? The locator device he had salvaged from the chopper—and disabled with the hope of throwing Zachary's men off course—contained a battery the same voltage as the chopper battery that was destroyed in the crash. Of course! He could use this battery to power the mobile phone he salvaged from the chopper. He knew the battery wasn't up to full potential since the device had been emitting its signal quite awhile before he disconnected it, and he knew the phone would put a stronger power drain on the battery, but with any luck he might get one call out. Wasting no time, he grabbed the phone, the black box containing the battery, the duct tape, and the tools. When his work was done, he ended up with a bulky, makeshift device that looked like pure junk but that just might work. His next question was, who should he call? Then he smiled. There was one man Tanner knew exactly where to find right now, and he knew the phone number by heart.

* * *

It had been a long, hard shift for Cory. Sitting behind a microphone required an upbeat attitude ever single second of airtime, something Cory seldom had a problem with, but today it had required his most difficult masquerade ever. It was all he could do to remain at work, knowing how hard Tanner's absence had to be on Katherine. Cory had just ended a commercial and signaled his engineer to start the next CD when the vibrator on his cell phone caught his attention. Removing the phone from his pocket, he saw the call was from an unknown number. Who could it be? Cory was careful about who he gave out this number to, and he had everyone on the list programmed into his caller ID. He finally concluded that whoever it was, they could wait. He'd had enough talking and trying to sound upbeat for the time being.

* * *

"Cory Harper, don't you dare ignore this call," Mitzi said in his ear, this time in more than just a whisper. "Answer that phone and answer it now, or you'll have one irate lady angel to deal with. And I happen to be on a first-name basis with your guardian angel, so I can make good on my promise."

Brandon did a double take. "I never heard you give a suggestion quite that strong, Mitzi."

"Well, you have now," she said through a beaming smile. "And look, it worked. He's answering Tanner's call."

* * *

Cory caught his engineer's attention and indicated he was about to take a call. He knew the man would cover for him if the call lasted longer than the CD. "Yeah, Cory Harper here," he said into the phone.

"Cory! Thank heavens you answered! It's me, Tanner!"

Cory leapt from his chair, eyes wide. "Tanner?! But I thought . . . ? Weren't you in a plane crash?"

"Plane crash? I don't know what you're talking about. Listen carefully to what I'm about to say because this phone could cut out any minute. This is no joke, it's a matter of life and death!"

"Shoot, buddy. I'm listening."

"I was hit with a tranquilizer dart while working in my lab last night. I woke up in a chopper that landed on a small island somewhere off the coast of Mexico, I'd guess."

"You'd guess? You don't know where it is?"

"No, Cory, I don't know where it is. And I'm using a mobile phone that can't be traced without special equipment. Zachary

Wagner is at the bottom of this. I found the proof, and I found proof he killed Brandon. In fact, I found Brandon's body."

"On the island?"

"Yeah!"

"This is heavy stuff! I talked with Katherine earlier. She told me about what you found at the cabin."

"Good, then you'll understand when I tell you it was Brandon's blood and fingerprints on the disk. Not only that, what was on the disk is enough to put Zachary Wagner away for the rest of his life. I'm afraid for Katie's life, Cory. Find her and make sure she's somewhere safe."

"Good as done!"

"And above all, keep Vince away from her!"

"You think Vince is one of them?"

"I'm not sure, but don't take any chances. I outsmarted the two dupes who brought me here. They won't be showing up for dinner tonight."

"Listen, Tanner, the world thinks you crashed your company jet somewhere in the ocean. You reportedly called in a distress call, then disappeared."

"That could explain why Conrad parachuted to the island," Tanner reasoned aloud.

"Huh?"

"Never mind, I'll explain later. Can you get your hands on a map showing small, uninhabited islands off the coast of the States and Mexico?"

"Can and will do! We'll find you, buddy! Hang in there!"

The answer came only as a garbled and indiscernible noise. "Hello, Tanner!" Cory shouted into the phone. "Are you still there?" This time there was no answer at all.

"Tanner's alive!" Cory shouted. "I've got my work cut out." Rushing from the sound studio and into the engineer's quarters, Cory shouted his intentions. "I have a big problem, buddy. Find a way to cover for me, okay?"

"You're covered, Cory," the engineer responded without the slightest hesitation. "But you owe me big-time!"

"You got it!" Cory called back, already halfway to the outside door, which he burst through, rushing straight to his car. Once he was on the road and heading for Alexis's house, where he expected Katherine to be, he punched Alexis's number with the intention of giving them a warning about Vincent. To his chagrin, all he got was Alexis's answering machine. Next he tried the hospital, where the receptionist informed him Alexis was working in the emergency room. "I've got to talk to her!" Cory insisted. "Tell her it's her brother!"

"She's really tied up at the moment. I don't think I should bother her."

"This is an emergency! Cory shouted. "Get her to the phone!"

"It'll take me a minute or two," the receptionist said.

"I'll wait, but hurry every chance you get!"

Not knowing where else to head, Cory changed direction with the idea of going to his own house. He had traveled barely three blocks when Alexis's voice came on the line. "What is it, Cory? I'm really tied up right now."

"Katherine could be in big trouble," Cory shot back. "Do you have any idea where she might be?"

"She was at home when I left for work, that's all I know. What kind of trouble?"

"I'll fill you in later. Right now I have a lot to do. But if you hear anything from her, call me fast, okay?"

"Wait!" his sister shouted. "As I was driving away, I saw Vincent's Lexus headed for the apartment. He'll probably know where she is."

"Oh, great," Cory mumbled to himself. "Thanks, Alexis. I'll get back when I know something. Call if you hear anything."

"You know I will. You have me worried, Cory. Tell me what this is about."

"All I can tell you right now is Tanner is alive. I talked with him not five minutes ago. But I really have to go. I promise to fill you in the first chance I get."

Cory hated doing it, but he hung up before Alexis could respond. He had to have time to think, to plan his course of action. Then he remembered that he was the one who told Vincent about Tanner's supposed plane crash. What had he done? He had sent a possible killer right to Katherine's doorstep.

* * *

"The Village Inn restaurant on Northern Avenue," Mitzi instructed. "And get there as fast as you can!"

* * *

"Village Inn?" Cory queried aloud. "This is no time to be thinking about food."

* * *

"Listen to me, Cory," Mitzi continued. "That restaurant is important for more reasons than food right now. Drive by it, and you'll find out for yourself why. I wasn't lying to you when I told you it was important to answer your cell phone, and I'm not lying now."

* * *

"The phone call from Tanner," Cory muttered. "It was like a voice in my mind told me to answer it. Now I hear voices telling me to drive by the Village Inn. You don't suppose . . . ?" Cory's chest rose and fell with sharp breaths. "But, just in case . . ."

He changed direction again, this time headed for Northern Avenue. Once he came to the parking lot entrance, he turned in with the intention of driving straight through, then heading home. But something caught his eye. It was a black Lexus SC 430. "That's Vince's car," he gasped. "But there's no one inside. Could Vince be in the restaurant? If so, is Katherine with him?"

Cory pulled into the spot next to the Lexus. He quickly got out of his car with the intention of checking inside the restaurant, but as he walked past the Lexus, what he saw instantly changed his mind. Vincent was slumped over in the front seat, apparently fast asleep. "Vince! Wake up!" Cory yelled, pounding on the window. There was no response. Vincent didn't even flinch. Cory yanked on the door, pulling it open. Grabbing Vincent by the shoulders, Cory shook him hard. "You're not just asleep," Cory stated as the realization set in. "You've been drugged, Vince!" Cory gave him a vigorous slap. "Wake up, man!"

"Whaa . . ." Vincent mumbled, trying to open his eyes.

Cory shook him again. "Snap out of it, Vince!"

"Ooooh," Vincent complained. "Who hit me . . . ?"

"You've been drugged. Fight it, Vince! You've got to wake up!"

"Cory, is that you . . . ?" Vincent was mumbling like he had a mouth full of cotton.

"It's me, Vince! Katherine is in trouble, and you may be the only one who can help her."

The mention of Katherine apparently triggered something in Vincent's foggy mind. His eyes rolled into a fixed focus, staring straight at Cory's face. "Katie," he mumbled. "Winston has her! . . . Harmon . . ." He slurred the last word out.

"Winston Harmon?" Cory asked loudly.

"Yes," Vincent managed. "Winston drugged Katie." Vincent's speech was still very slurred, but he was beginning to make some sense at least. "When I tried to stop Winston, he jabbed me with a needle."

Cory could only wonder if this was all just an act of a guilty man trying to cover the truth, or if it was it genuine concern. Seeing a friend like Vincent through the eyes of an accuser was so foreign to Cory he wondered if remaining blind might not be the better course. Regardless of his feelings for Vincent, he had little choice but to put the truth on the table. "I'm sorry to tell you this, Vince, but Winston's not the main force behind Katherine's disappearance. That honor belongs to your daddy."

"Not you too, Cory!" Vincent snapped. "Where are you people coming up with this rubbish?"

"It's not rubbish, Vince. It's documented fact. I learned it from Tanner, who's still very much alive, by the way."

Vincent's eyes shot open. "Alive?! Are you sure?"

"I talked with him not more than an hour ago."

"But . . . ? What about the plane crash?"

"There was no plane crash, at least not one with Tanner onboard. It's more of your father's doing, Vince, and Tanner has the evidence to prove it."

Anger blazed from Vincent's eyes. "By evidence are you referring to that computer disk and those splotches of blood that supposedly came from father's office?"

"Tanner used DNA to prove the blood was Brandon's. And on the disk, he found irrefutable evidence involving your father. I know how much you love your father, but the facts speak for themselves."

"Who else knows about this?" Vincent asked sharply.

"As far as I know I'm the only one, other than Tanner."

Vincent rubbed his eyes. "Where is Tanner?" he asked.

"I'm not exactly sure, and neither was he. It seems two of your father's men broke into his lab and drugged him the same way they drugged you and Katherine. They took him to a small island he assumed was somewhere off the coast of Mexico."

"Conrad and Franco," Vincent angrily vented. "It had to be them."

"Well, you won't have to worry about those two anymore. Tanner turned the tables on them."

"They're dead?"

"That's what he said."

"The island," Vincent continued. "Tell me more about it."

"Not much to tell. Tanner described it as small and uninhabited. And there's one thing I haven't mentioned yet. Tanner found Brandon's body."

Vincent stepped from the car and took several deep breaths. What he said next caught Cory by complete surprise. "I may know where the island is, Cory."

"What? Vince, you're not involved in this, are you?"

Vincent shook his head. "First my father, and now me? I lost a logbook some time back, and I suspected Winston might have found it since it would be just like Winston to hide the book until he felt bringing it to light might serve some useful purpose in his conniving little mind. Winston is good at that sort of thing. Anyway, I let myself into his office and searched his desk. I found the logbook and noticed a map lying next to it. It was a map of the coast off Mexico, and someone had circled a small island several miles off shore. The map struck me as odd, since as far as I knew, Wagner Aerospace had no connection with any such island. I figured Winston had personal reasons for pinpointing it on the map, and if he was using company time and resources for something personal, I reasoned that knowing about the map might give me some ammunition if and when he ever tried to pull one of his shenanigans on me again. I made a copy of the map. It's in my desk back at the hangar." Vincent dug a set of keys out of his pocket. "Here," he said, handing them to Cory. "We'll take my car; it's faster. But you'll have to drive. My head's not up to it."

"I need to call my family, Vince. I don't want them wondering where I am."

"You can call them from my office while I get the map and fire us up some transportation."

Cory took the keys and shoved them in the ignition. "To Falcon Field, I presume?"

"Just as fast as you can get us there, friend."

* * *

Tanner could only wonder how much good the call to Cory had done. There wasn't much time to get a message out, and he had no way of giving Cory a location for this island. He could only hope Cory would be able to keep Katherine out of Zachary's hands. That was the important thing now. As for Tanner, there was no reason he couldn't survive on this island as long as necessary. There were plenty of roots he could eat, and he figured he'd be able to catch crabs and small sea life off the rocks close to shore. Fire wouldn't be a problem for an experienced camper like him.

"Please don't let them hurt Katie," he whispered. "Take me if you will, but don't let them hurt Katie."

CHAPTER 23

Katherine's head pounded. She'd had headaches before, but never one like this. She wanted to rub her eyes, but she couldn't make her hands work. They were in her lap, and she was wearing bracelets—awful, awful bracelets. Where did she get those things? She tried to remember but couldn't. All she could remember was watching an old movie about Vincent. No, it wasn't about Vincent, it was about a man with a sharp needle. Her eyes suddenly shot open as she remembered the man in the black suit. It wasn't only her head that hurt, it was her neck too, where he had jabbed her with a needle. She looked down. Those weren't bracelets, they were . . . "Why am I ha-a-a- . . . ?" The word *handcuffed* hung in her mouth.

"Welcome back, Miss Dalton."

She felt a start. Whoever had spoken was in the seat next to her. His voice sounded hollow, like an old phonograph record played at slow speed. *Wake up, wake up,* Katherine told herself over and over in her haze-filled mind. *Make this fog go away and wake up!* She narrowed her eyes, trying to focus. Who was this man? It wasn't Vincent, and it wasn't the man in the black suit. He was someone she should know, but who? With great effort, she managed a question. "Who *are* you?"

The man's voice was somewhat clearer now, but not a lot. "I see no reason for not answering your question at this point, Miss Dalton. I'm Zachary Wagner, your friend Vincent's father."

The name hit with sobering impact. Katherine had never met Zachary Wagner, but she had seen him on the news numerous times. Realizing she was in his clutches worked miracles at clearing her mind. "Why am I wearing these?" she said, holding up her cuffed hands.

"The cuffs are merely a precaution. You see, Miss Dalton, I'm not used to handling this sort of thing myself. The men I usually depend on for such matters have left my organization, so to speak. You have no idea how badly I feel about you stumbling onto information you had no business seeing. I'm entirely aware of my son's feelings for you, and I had hoped someday to welcome you into the family. Killing you is going to bring me great pain, but, my dear, it would seem you leave me no other choice."

"You murdered Brandon," she said. "And Tanner? You've murdered him, haven't you?"

"They left me no choice, Miss Dalton. Though I must admit, killing them was easier than killing you will be. You see, Brandon and Tanner both offered my son competition when it came to your affections. Removing them from the game had a double advantage."

"A game?" Katherine shot back.

"All life is a game, my dear. There are winners and there are losers. Sometimes being a winner requires bending the rules. It's the smart player who figures that out early on."

The pilot spoke up. "That's the island just up ahead, Mr. Wagner. We'll be on the ground in about five minutes." Katherine couldn't be certain, as all she could see of the pilot was his profile, but she strongly suspected he was the man in the black suit. "I haven't flown one of these things in years," the pilot continued. "But it's like they say about riding a bicycle. You never forget."

"You're doing just fine, Winston," Zachary assured the man. "We may have to think about renewing your license until we can make other arrangements."

Katherine had no idea what this conversation was about other than the part about her life being in danger. She had always heard that someone facing death would have their entire life flash before their eyes, but it wasn't so in her case. The only thing in her mind right now was finding a way out.

Zachary pointed through the window. "You see that beautiful little island up ahead, Miss Dalton? That will become your final resting place. A very lovely spot, don't you agree?"

"You're a monster," Katherine declared. "You have no conscience."

"Please, Miss Dalton, no theatrics. Life is what it is. I'm simply one of the players who understands the rules better than most." Katherine sank lower in her seat as a feeling of complete helplessness tightened around her.

She had endured rough landings before, but nothing like the one when this pilot touched down on the island beach. He had claimed to be rusty at the controls, and he wasn't lying. Once they were on the ground, Zachary removed her handcuffs. "I see no reason to force any unnecessary discomfort on you, Miss Dalton," Exiting the chopper, he turned and offered her a hand. "May I?" he asked with sickening politeness.

Katherine shoved his hand aside and stepped out on her own. "I hope you realize how truly sorry I am that things have come down to this, Miss Dalton," he explained. "I take no joy in your demise. If it's any comfort, they say drowning is actually quite painless."

"You are a monster!" she spit out. "You're about to add me to a list of who knows how many other murders, and you think I should be grateful because you've chosen a way for me to die easy? You're a sick, heartless man! Someone will bring you down, and when you fall, it's going to be hard!"

"Say what you will, Miss Dalton. But I've designed the perfect—hopefully you'll forgive the crudeness of my name for it—execution chamber here on this island. I'll never be found out. To the eyes of the world, I'll remain the respectable and highly successful businessman they've come to know me as. When the sun comes up tomorrow morning, I'll be enjoying breakfast as usual."

Zachary removed the pistol from his belt and cocked the breech, injecting a shell into the chamber. "Just a precaution," he explained. Then he instructed Winston, "Stay with the chopper. Miss Dalton and I will only be a moment." Winston, whom Katherine was now certain was the man who had drugged her, signaled his understanding.

"This way, my dear," Zachary said, taking hold of Katherine's arm.

"You may think you've gotten away with your little game," Katherine boldly stated as they walked, "but you're wrong. You made a mistake when you came up against a man like Tanner Nelson.

Tanner was on to you, and I promise you, he figured out a way to let someone know what he found. Count on it."

"That makes a nice story, Miss Dalton, but not one that will hold water. All the evidence Tanner found has been destroyed."

Zachary suddenly froze in his tracks. "What the . . . ?!" he gasped. "How did this happen?"

Katherine instantly picked up on his concern and glanced over. What looked like pieces of a large boulder littered the ground outside the entrance to a cave. "Well, now," she said, taking courage. "Do we have a problem?"

Zachary didn't answer but pressed on to the cave, where he leaned in for a look. "How can this be?" He shook his head. "It makes no sense!"

At that instant, the air was shattered by the sound of a tremendous explosion. Whirling around, Zachary suddenly turned ash gray. "The chopper," he gasped, seeing it in flames. "What's happened?"

Katherine felt her heart leap as she reasoned what this had to mean. Tanner was alive. "If you're planning to drown me, this is a strange way to go about it," she prodded.

Zachary swallowed and wiped the sweat from his brow.

"Tanner!" Katherine cried out. "Come and get me! I'm growing tired of bad company!"

"Shut up!" Zachary snapped, gripping Katherine's arm tighter and forcing her back in the direction of the blazing chopper. "Winston!" he bellowed. "Where are you?"

A muffled sound from overhead caught both Katherine's and Zachary's attention. Looking up, they spotted Winston dangling by a rope tossed over the stem of a palm frond. He was halfway up the tree, bound and gagged with duct tape. It was all Katherine could do to keep from laughing at the sight of him. "Oops," she jabbed. "Looks like Winston's learned for himself that Tanner's alive. I guess that means you're next in line for the lesson, Mr. Wagner."

Sweat dripped from Zachary's brow into his eyes, causing him to blink. "Shut up!" he barked, removing a cell phone from his blazer pocket. "I'm still in charge here as long as I have you where I can put a bullet in your skull!"

Zachary was doing a juggling act, trying to hold Katherine, the gun, and dial the phone all at the same time. Katherine was wise enough to know he didn't dare kill her now, not with her being his only ticket out of this predicament. She made a quick decision, and in a lightning-fast move, she yanked the phone from his hand and heaved it into the flaming helicopter.

"You little witch!" Zachary bellowed. "You'll pay for that!"

"Losing our temper, are we?" she asked, refusing to let up. "They say losing your temper only makes you reason less clearly. Quite personally, I'd think you'd want a clear mind right now."

Zachary wiped his brow. "I know you're out there, Tanner!" he yelled. "But this little show of yours has gone on long enough. Show yourself or I'll kill the girl right now!" Placing the barrel of the gun against Katherine's head, he added, "I mean it! Show yourself!" Katherine realized that Zachary was noticeably trembling.

A rock struck the top of a palm tree, then fell to the ground, pulling Zachary's attention to a spot near them. He strained for a look. "What the?" he gasped. "Is that . . . ?"

Refusing to lower his gun, he forced Katherine ahead of him as he moved in for a closer look. "It's Conrad's chopper," he muttered at the discovery. "They never made it off the island."

"Now you know," came a voice from behind them, a voice Katherine instantly knew to be Tanner's. She spun to see him standing beside a large rock about twenty-five feet up the side of a small mountain. She instantly realized he had thrown the rock to lure Zachary over to this wreckage. Shoving Katherine aside, Zachary raised his gun and fired off two shots, which only ricocheted harmlessly away as Tanner easily ducked behind the rock. "So help me, Tanner," Zachary demanded. "If you don't show yourself, I will kill her!"

Tanner replied with confidence, "Katie's your shield, Wagner. Lose your shield and you'll never get off this island alive. By the way, Katie, thanks for depriving Wagner of his cell phone. I figured on having to do that myself."

"Glad I could help," she half laughed and half sobbed.

"Take a look at your cohort dangling from that tree," Tanner continued. "There's something taped to his shirt. Can you make out what it is?"

"A cell phone!" Zachary barked.

"Very good. Now think about this, Wagner. That cell phone could be your only ticket off this island. But it might be a little more difficult for you to get than just climbing up a tree. You see, I've tucked away an explosive inside your fellow's pocket. I have my thumb against a detonator that can send both him and the phone into orbit with one little push. Care to talk trade? Your cohort and the phone for Katie?"

Zachary's eyes narrowed. "You're bluffing," he spit back. "Where would you get access to explosives?"

"Where, indeed?" Tanner calmly answered. "How else could I have brought down the chopper you're standing next to or disintegrated the stone covering the entrance to your execution chamber? I'm growing impatient with this conversation, Wagner. Do we talk trade, or do I press this detonator?"

"No! Don't destroy the cell phone! We'll talk!"

"How touching," Tanner laughed. "So much concern for your man's safety. Here's the way we do this. You release Katie and let her walk to me. When she reaches the large rock face just below me, I'll toss the detonator onto the beach."

Katherine sized up the situation. Even if she did reach the face of the rock surface below Tanner, getting up that surface would take some doing. He'd have to lean over as far as possible, she'd have to jump up, and the two would have to use all their combined energies to pull her to safety. What would keep Zachary from shooting her as soon as Tanner tossed the detonator to the beach? From the look on Zachary's face, she knew he was thinking along the same lines. The answer to her concern came with Tanner's next declaration.

"I didn't mention the detonator has a timing device on it, did I? I'll set the timer for ten seconds. That should give you sufficient time to retrieve it and figure out how the disarming mechanism works."

"Ten seconds?" Zachary gasped. "That's absurd! I need more time!"

"All right, I'll make it twenty. Provided you lay your gun down before we begin."

"Thirty seconds!" Zachary demanded, the sweat beading on his brow.

"Put the gun down, and I'll give you thirty seconds."

Very slowly, Zachary bent down and lay the gun on the sand close to his feet.

"Okay, now let Katie step far enough away so you can't grab her."

"No more than three steps," Zachary growled. "Or I'll retrieve the gun and kill her on the spot."

Katherine didn't hesitate. She pulled free from Zachary's hold and moved forward three very large steps. "Hold it!" Zachary shouted. "No further! Not until I see that detonator!"

Tanner emerged from behind the rock. "Are we ready to do this?" he asked.

"Throw down the detonator," Zachary barked.

"On the count of three," Tanner instructed. "When you hear me say three, run faster than you've ever run before, Katie. You got that?"

"Yes," she nervously agreed.

"One . . ."

Katherine drew an anxious breath and glanced back to see Zachary's hand reaching out toward the gun. She knew he wouldn't leave the gun behind, but she could only hope he'd be worried enough about reaching the detonator in time not to take a shot right away.

"Two . . ." Tanner called out confidently. Then, catching both Katherine and Zachary off guard, he said, "I lied about the extra time. The detonator is set for twenty seconds. Three!" He tossed an object into the wake of an incoming wave. Katherine broke for the rock as Zachary's grunt told her he had grabbed the gun and was headed for the detonator.

* * *

"This is unbearable," Brandon moaned. "All we can do is stand here watching. Why didn't the authorities give me an angelic zap gun so I could help save her?"

"Angelic zap gun?" Mitzi laughed. "Angels don't use guns."

"How about a sword? Everyone knows angels can use swords when the authorities decree."

"You're not that kind of angel, Brandon. Trust me, Tanner and Katherine will be fine."

"We both know Tanner's bomb is a bluff. What's to keep the jerk from shooting her?"

"Zachary doesn't know it's a bluff. Look at him. All he's interested in is doing whatever possible to save that cell phone. Won't he be surprised when he finds nothing but a rock?"

Brandon looked to see Mitzi was right. Zachary was frantically splashing through the water on his hands and knees while Katherine had already reached the rock where Tanner waited. But he still couldn't help worrying. After all, Zachary did have the gun.

"Anyone ever tell you you're cute when you're worried?" Mitzi remarked.

Brandon's jaw dropped as he turned to look at her. "The world is falling apart and you pick *now* to tell me I'm cute?" he said, aghast.

"Well, you are. A little lacking in faith, yes, but cute all the same. Take a breath and settle down. Everything is going to be fine."

Brandon could only marvel at this lovely angel's faith and wisdom. How could Katherine and Tanner not come out fine with Mitzi Palmer in their corner? Brandon suddenly felt very warm inside. And he liked it.

* * *

"Jump, Katie, grab my hand!" Tanner's words echoed through Katherine's mind as she focused every ounce of energy into doing just that. Never slowing, she hurled herself upward to feel her hand fall into his powerful grip. A heartbeat later, she was in his arms as he whispered, "It's okay, Katie. You're safe now."

"I thought you were dead," she sobbed in relief.

She felt him laugh. "I was still kicking last time I checked." He eased her back a step and wiped her face with his handkerchief. "How you doing?" he asked. "You okay?"

"I'm okay," she sniffed.

"Good. We have to get you higher up in the rocks before Zachary figures out I was lying about the explosive."

Crouching low, Tanner led the way to a point where he felt she would be safe. "What about that other cell phone?" Katherine asked. "Is it real?"

"It's real enough, but I have the battery in my pocket. Now, listen to me, Katie. I want you to stay right here. No matter what happens, don't show yourself. Do you understand?"

"What are you going to do?" she asked,

"I'm going to try to lure Wagner into the rain forest to even the playing field. He has a gun, and I don't. I had hoped to take one from the guy I hung in the tree, but he wasn't carrying one."

"I'm going with you," Katherine insisted. "You'll need my help."

"You are *not* going with me, Katie Dalton. You are going to stay right here where you'll be out of sight and as safe as I can make you from that madman."

"There's that stubborn streak again. You always have to have the last word, and you always have to be right."

"I'm not being stubborn, I'm using common sense. Now stay put!"

Katherine didn't like it, but she backed down. She watched with no small measure of concern as Tanner moved out of the rocks and slipped into the darkness of the rain forest. "I might consider marrying you sometime if it wasn't for that stubborn streak," she mumbled. "Of course you haven't asked me yet. Probably because you're too darn stubborn to admit you're in love with me."

CHAPTER 24

Gripping his pistol in one hand, Zachary frantically waded through the shallow surf, looking for the detonator. "Curse you, Tanner Nelson!" he spat out in his fury. "How have you done this to me?"

Zachary's hand struck something hard, which he yanked from the water. "A rock!" he bellowed, throwing it back down. "There is no detonator! I've been deceived!"

Scrambling to his feet, Zachary stared up at Winston. "There's no explosive either! You will pay for this, Mr. Nelson."

Zachary searched the rocks, but just as he suspected, there was no one to be seen by this time. "What kind of man are you?" Zachary growled. "What's it going to take to bring you down?"

Zachary cautiously moved to the palm tree where Winston hung suspended. Aiming his gun at the point where the rope was tied, he fired off a shot. The rope snapped, and Winston fell with a thud at Zachary's feet. Zachary ripped the cell phone from Winston's chest. "It's dead!" he shouted. "Tanner's taken the battery!"

Zachary shoved the phone into his pocket, then reached down and yanked the tape away from Winston's mouth.

"There's a knife in my left pocket!" Winston shouted. "Cut me loose!"

Zachary pulled out the knife and had Winston loose within seconds. "You fool!" Zachary exclaimed. "How did you let this happen?"

"I never saw him coming. He had me before I knew it," Winston said, rubbing the skin where the tape had been.

"He didn't take a gun from you?" Zachary asked worriedly.

"You know me, I never use a gun. I leave that part to guys like Conrad and Franco."

Zachary rubbed his chin. "At least he's not armed. We've got to get that battery, Winston. No one even knows where we are. If we don't get this cell phone working, we could die here."

"We're two men with a pistol against an unarmed man and a girl," Winston reminded him. "We will get that battery, and while we're at it, I have a score to settle with Mr. Nelson."

Zachary handed Winston back his knife while looking around for any telltale sign that might hint at Tanner's whereabouts. "Don't count this man out just yet," he warned. "He's a clever one. The last thing we want to do is confront him inside that rain forest. We have to find a way to lure him out here."

"How are we supposed to do that, Mr. Wagner? Time is on his side, not ours."

Zachary threw a nervous glance toward the rain forest. "Yeah, you're right, time is on his side. If it comes down to a question of survival, everything we'd need is in there, not here on the beach. This pistol is our equalizer. I've used three shots; that leaves six more in the clip. However we do this, we're going to have to be darn sure not to waste another shot."

Suddenly, an unexpected sound caught both men's attention. "Look!" Zachary cried. "It's a chopper, and it's coming this way! I think it's one of ours!"

"It is one of ours," Winston agreed as the craft neared. "Who is it?"

"It has to be Mel Phillips," Zachary returned. "He's the last pilot we have other than my son."

"Yeah, that makes sense. Mel knows about this island, and he knows Conrad and Franco are missing. I wouldn't put it past him to pull something like this." Winston laughed. "Under any other circumstance, I'd have his neck."

"How does Mel know these things?" Zachary asked, surprised at hearing this.

"I sent Mel out looking for Conrad and Franco. In retrospect I see I should never have done it."

"No, Winston, you did right. How could Mel have found us otherwise?"

The two men moved to the center of the beach. "How we going to handle this?" Winston asked. "We have to be careful about how much we let Mel figure out."

"We'll just have to see to it that Mel never leaves the island. He can stay here and rot with the rest of them."

"I don't like it, Mr. Wagner. What if they happened to be discovered?"

"Good point, Winston. I'll hire a professional to come back and finish the job. You can fly them here later and dump all the bodies in the ocean. That way, we'll have covered all our tracks." Zachary glanced up. "Right now we have to make sure Mel spots us."

The two men began shouting and waving.

* * *

"There!" Cory noted, pointing at the tiny spot on the ocean ahead of them. "There is an island, just like the map indicates. But where's the smoke coming from? Is it a signal fire?"

"It's no signal fire," Vincent said. "It's a downed craft. And there's two guys on the beach signaling to us."

"It's your father, Vince. And isn't that guy with him one of your men?"

"Winston Harmon. No wonder that chopper ended up in a pile of smoke if Winston was at the controls. Winston hasn't flown in years. If Dad needed a pilot, why in the name of good sense didn't he come to me?"

Cory glanced at Vincent and chose his words carefully. "Your father came here to murder Katherine, Vince. Would he have wanted you along for that?"

"You're jumping to conclusions, Cory! I can't think of any reason Winston would have taken Katie the way he did, but it doesn't necessarily mean he brought her here. There's no sign of her down there."

"Katherine's there somewhere, you can bet on it. And so is Tanner! You better pray they're not inside that downed chopper."

Vincent wiped his brow, which Cory noticed was beaded with sweat. "Let's say you're right about the blood on that disk and about it containing incriminating evidence. Why does my father have to be the one under suspicion?"

"What's your point?" Cory asked.

"My point is that it was Winston who drugged me and grabbed Katie. Who's to say he hasn't been putting something over on my father? Believe me, Cory, my father's not capable of killing people."

"It's possible, I suppose. But regardless, our main concern right now has to be Katherine and Tanner. They need our help, and we have little choice but to assume both your father and this Winston are the enemy. If we let down our guard and learn too late we're wrong, it could spell disaster."

Cory reached for the radio mike and was about to key it when Vincent cut him off. "What are you doing?" he snapped.

"What do you think? I'm calling the coast guard!"

"No! You can't do that! That would bring in the media, and you of all people should know how things get blown out of proportion once the media get involved. We'll handle this ourselves."

Cory ignored Vincent and keyed the mike. Before he could speak, Vincent unsnapped the connector at the radio. "No coast guard, Cory! You can give me that much!"

"This is crazy, Vince! We're not qualified to do this alone. Let me make that call!"

"No! We do this my way!"

Cory glanced down at the two men on the beach. "I hate to bring this up, Vince, but your father's the one with the gun."

"Maybe my father's taken Winston captive."

"And maybe flies don't swarm around spilt syrup. I want to know, Vince, is your head just buried in the sand, or are you part of the problem?"

"I'm going to pretend I didn't hear that," Vincent grumbled.

"Don't get coy with me. You have to admit you've been acting pretty darn suspicious about this. I know your loyalty to your father, but wake up and smell the gunpowder."

"All right, Cory. I guess I can't blame you for thinking what you might."

"Can I call the coast guard?"

"Let me land and see what's going on for sure. You can call them if anything goes wrong."

* * *

Hearing an approaching chopper, Tanner moved quickly to the edge of the beach for a better look. "Wouldn't you know it," he huffed. "It's one of Zachary's. Talk about going from the frying pan to the fire." Tanner glanced up at the rocks to make certain Katherine was still out of sight. So far so good. All he could do was sit tight and see where things went next.

CHAPTER 25

"That's not Mel!" Zachary gasped in shock as the chopper came into plain view. "It's Vincent!"

"And he has a passenger," Wagner added.

"It's his friend Cory Harper!" Zachary spun to face Winston. "You didn't let Vince see you grab Katherine, did you?"

Winston ran a hand nervously through his hair. "I couldn't help it, Mr. Wagner. The two of them were together, and I had no way to separate them. I should have drugged Vincent first and then grabbed the woman."

"You drugged my son?" Zachary bellowed.

"I had no choice, Mr. Wagner! It was the only way!"

"You fool! You know my orders were to keep Vincent out of this! He knows you took her, and he's somehow traced you here to this island. How am I ever going to keep him from finding out what's going on? I told you I wanted it to appear as though she was on the plane with Tanner when he crashed into the ocean, and all the time you knew that wouldn't work since Vincent saw you grab her!"

"Maybe we can make him believe we brought her here looking for Tanner's downed plane and that she was killed in the chopper crash."

Zachary considered this. It was a long shot, but thanks to Winston's bungling, it was all he had. "We can't let him see inside the wreckage," Zachary said. "We'll have to convince him to get off this island the fastest way possible." He felt as if his mind would explode as he watched the chopper touch down.

* * *

Vincent turned off the engine and shoved the radio mike under his seat and out of Cory's reach. All the aircraft in Zachary Wagner's fleet were outfitted with an automatic pistol holstered on the pilot's door. Vincent pulled this from its holster and shoved it under his belt. Opening the door, he hopped out onto the beach. "Thank heavens you're here, son," Zachary said, deliberately blocking Vincent's way to the downed chopper. "There's been a terrible accident, and Winston's been hurt badly. Get back in the chopper, son, we have to get him to a hospital fast!"

Vincent glanced at Winston, who looked perfectly healthy. "No games, Father. Tell me straight out, what have you done with Katie?"

Zachary laid a hand on Vincent's shoulder. "I'm so sorry, son. Katherine didn't make it." He motioned toward the wreckage. "It's not pretty. Come on, let's get Winston to a doctor. I'll send someone back to take care of things here."

In spite of his father's efforts to stop him, Vincent forced his way around. "I want a look for myself," he said.

"No!" Zachary shouted, grabbing Vincent's arm. "There's nothing you can do for her!"

Vincent broke free and ran toward the wreckage.

* * *

This was the very distraction Cory was hoping for. Fishing the mike out from under the seat, he hurriedly attached it to the radio. The sound of a gunshot pulled his attention back to Zachary, who now leveled the barrel of the gun straight at him. "That shot was just to get your attention," Zachary warned. "Step away from that chopper, now!"

Cory dropped the mike, but, spotting the keys still in the ignition, formulated a hurried plan. Carefully he eased them out and slipped them into his pocket. As he exited the chopper, he spotted Vincent lying on the beach, his head bleeding after apparently being struck by a rock still in Winston's hand.

"You idiot!" Zachary shouted at Winston once he had Cory restrained. "Why did you hit my son?"

"He'll be fine," Winston responded. "Other than a headache. I had to do something. Once he had seen inside the wreckage he would have been impossible to deal with. Let me tie him up and put him in the chopper while you dispose of this one."

Zachary wet his lips. "This thing is getting more complicated by the minute. How many more people do we have to kill? And how can I ever square things with my son?"

"We'll think of something, but we can't let this one go, and we need to restrain your son before he comes to."

Cory's eyes darted around at what sounded like the call of a mockingbird. This was a signal he and the other four musketeers had devised between themselves back in their college days. Tanner was alive, and he was out there in that forest trying to catch Cory's attention. It took only a second for Cory to spot him behind a clump of vines. Cory had to bite his lip to keep quiet. Tanner held up his hand, revealing a small rock. Using gestures, he got the message across that he wanted Cory to make a break for it when he used the rock as a distraction. Cory nodded slightly.

A well-aimed throw bounced the rock off the side of the chopper. Both Zachary and Winston spun to see what had happened just as Cory dashed for the rainforest, running a zigzag pattern just in case Zachary might shoot. Two shots did ring out, but not before Cory heard a cry of pain followed by a streak of swear words. Cory dove for cover and rolled onto the ground behind the trunk of a large palm tree. "Over here, and hurry," Tanner called.

Cory spotted him and dashed the last few yards. "What was all that ruckus back there?" he asked, trying to catch his breath.

"That was Zachary," Tanner explained. "I hit him in the head with a rock just as he was about to shoot. I thought about not doing it after your little game on the radio yesterday."

"Sorry about that, man. But all's fair in . . . oh, you know. It was only right you share a little of Katherine's time with Vince." Cory took out the chopper keys and tossed them to Tanner. "Will this get me off your hook?"

"You grabbed the keys?" Tanner grinned. "Way to go, Cory."

"Where's Katherine?" Cory asked anxiously.

"Over there in those rocks," Tanner said, pointing. "I only tell you that because you're not sitting at your mike. Who knows what kind of contest you might conjure up for anyone finding her there."

"I'm telling you, we have to get out of here, Mr. Wagner," Winston said loud enough for Tanner and Cory to hear. "If you won't tie him up, at least get him in the chopper while I get it started."

"Uh-oh," Cory said. "Someone's about to discover the missing keys. I hope they don't think Vincent has them in his pocket, because if they look there, they're bound to find the pistol tucked inside his belt."

"Let's see if we can do something to distract them," Tanner said. "Stay down, Cory, and leave this to me." Tanner stepped forward just far enough to put himself in plain view. Holding up the chopper keys, he called out. "Hello, boys! Missing something? Like the keys to your chopper, perhaps?"

"He's not bluffing," Winston called to Zachary. "The keys are gone!"

Zachary glared at Tanner, his anger well beyond the boiling point. "I want you, Tanner!" he bellowed. "One way or another, I'm going to spit on your grave!"

"Over there!" Winston suddenly pointed and said. "In those rocks! Isn't it . . . ?"

"Oh, no," Tanner moaned. Katherine had managed to reveal her hiding place. "I told her to stay down."

"Well, Mr. Nelson," Zachary smirked. "Isn't this an interesting turn of events?"

CHAPTER 26

Katherine could have kicked herself. How could she have been so careless as to let them see her? She just wanted to know what was going on. Was that really so unreasonable? This sort of thing might be an everyday event for Tanner, but not for her. One minute she was being held prisoner, the next minute Tanner set her free, then came a chopper from out of nowhere with Vincent and Cory on board, and Zachary began shooting, Vincent was knocked out, Cory ran for cover while dodging bullets—it was enough to make anyone's head spin. Why shouldn't she be allowed to grab a peek, and how was she to know fate would turn Winston's head in her direction at the most inopportune moment? The question now was, what to do next? She didn't know her way around well enough to make a run for it. She'd just have to sit tight and hope for the best. Just then, Tanner's voice forced her to look.

"Wagner! It's not Katherine you want, it's me!"

Katherine looked on in horror at the panorama unfolding before her. Zachary and Winston were walking in her direction and had covered about half the distance when Tanner moved out into the open. "There are some things we need to discuss!" Tanner propositioned.

Katherine's eyes shifted to the gun in Zachary's hand. She knew he wouldn't hesitate using it if he could get off a good shot. Katherine's father had always been a bit of a gun buff who liked spending time at the shooting range. He had taken Katherine along on several occasions, enough for her to become quite familiar with certain firearms, such as the one Zachary now held. She knew it was an automatic with a nine-shot clip. According to her count, Zachary had fired off six shots so far, leaving him with only three. At the distance between him and Tanner, getting off an accurate shot would be a gamble. Katherine was sure Tanner was banking on this very thing.

"What's on your mind, Tanner?" Zachary asked, his voice low and cunning.

"I was thinking about that little secret of yours," Tanner continued. "You know, the one you've kept so neatly swept under the rug."

Katherine noticed Zachary stiffen at hearing this. "I don't know what you're talking about," he refuted.

"Oh, I think you know what I'm talking about. The secret that concerns certain, shall we say, unethical business practices at Wagner Aerospace."

"You're out of your mind, Tanner!"

"Am I? Maybe you'll think I'm out of my mind when I explain that your secret isn't a secret anymore."

This brought a burst of laughter as Zachary abandoned his futile attempt at denial. "That's where you're wrong, Tanner," he stated arrogantly. "My men found your computer and the floppy disk. Close, but no cigar. Everything's been erased."

Tanner's expression eased into a taunting grin. "Has it, Zachary? Or did I find a way to slip the information past your dupes before they got their hands on the evidence?"

"Impossible!" Zachary barked.

"Let me ask you a question. Have you ever heard the song *By The Time I Get To Phoenix?* Because if you have, you should know that the song has strong implications for your present situation. You see, Zachary, by the time you get to Phoenix, you'll find some big changes in your world as you know it. You're going to be quite the celebrity."

"Your lies will get you nowhere, Tanner."

"Let me explain something that you might have overlooked. Dealing with men like your Conrad is second nature to me. It's what I do. Now, I'm going to tell you a story, and I'd like you to picture it in your mind as we go along. I'm working in my lab at my computer. I've just discovered some very interesting things about how you run Wagner Aerospace, as well as about what really happened to Brandon Cheney. Now, picture someone showing up outside my door with the intention of breaking it open. Let's say it's Conrad. So, what do I do, Zachary? Do I just sit there wondering who it might be? Or do I take action?"

The look on Zachary's face left little doubt as to what was going on in his mind. Tanner had his undivided attention. He continued his explanation. "I only had about thirty seconds to act, but it was time enough, thanks to certain preprogramed addresses in my computer's mail system. I simply fired off a blanket e-mail. Oh, and did I mention I included an attachment? Care to guess what was in the attachment?"

"You're lying!" a now-shaken Zachary reaccused.

"I don't think so. Let's see, whose names were included in that blanket address? Oh yes, it was every lawyer who works for the Branson and Willard law firm. Ten of them altogether. All of them are smart enough to figure out what the unexpected mail in their box is all about, and they all know exactly how to handle just such a situation." Tanner glanced at his watch. "By now, I figure at least eight of the ten have checked their mail." Tanner's smile expanded. "It's like I say, Zachary. By the time you get to Phoenix, you're going to be a real celebrity."

* * *

Zachary felt his mouth go dry. Tanner might be bluffing, but something about the man's demeanor told Zachary he was telling the truth. How could any of this be happening? Zachary had worked so hard getting Wagner Aerospace to the point where it was now, and he had done it all for Vincent. It wasn't fair that this man who had always stood between Vincent and the woman he loved should now be standing between Vincent and all the plans Zachary had so carefully laid out for him.

Zachary did have a backup plan, but it was a plan he desperately hoped would never become necessary. To his deepest regret, it would appear it had. For years, Zachary had been using assumed names to hide away vast amounts of money in bank accounts all over the world. He'd taken great pains to ensure nothing could ever be traced back to him. He was ready, at a moment's notice, to vanish from sight and never be heard from again. He could live out his life in comfort and set up his son's future from behind the scenes. It would mean never being with his son again, or ever seeing his own grandchildren—a painful price that could be attributed to one man: Tanner Nelson. Even now, with Zachary giving in to this secondary plan, Tanner Nelson stood squarely in the way. Tanner held the key to the only transportation off this island.

Zachary weighed his options. The rules had changed. Everything centered around the keys to that chopper. Zachary knew it was Cory who had grabbed the keys, but he suspected Tanner had them now. Regardless of who had them, Tanner was the greatest threat and the one who had to be taken out first. Neither Cory nor the girl would present much problem with Tanner out of the way. Zachary felt his heart quicken, and he wet his lips. He couldn't chance a shot from this distance. Tightening his grip on the pistol, he inched forward a step.

* * *

Tanner had learned long ago to watch the eyes of an opponent. By doing this, he could predict a person's intentions with a high degree of accuracy. What he saw in Zachary was a man backed so deeply in a corner that reason had given way to desperation. Zachary's world was crumbling around him, and he was throwing caution and common sense to the wind. Tanner knew why Zachary was trying to close the gap; he only had three shots left. Tanner painstakingly calculated just how far he could let Zachary go before making his own move. It had come down to a battle of nerves, and Tanner was counting on nerves being the deciding element. Once the action began, it would be easier dodging the bullets of a frustrated man than one with a clear mind. Tension mounted as Zachary moved forward another step. Off in the distance, a wave broke over the already-damp sand. Overhead, a seagull called out to its mate. Tanner's eyes never shifted from Zachary's.

* * *

The report of a gun sent chills through Katherine. A second shot sounded almost instantly. Jumping to her feet, she spotted Zachary with a raised gun and Tanner down on one knee. "NO!" she screamed, scrambling down from the rocks toward the beach.

CHAPTER 27

The gun felt heavy in Zachary's hand. Had his bullet struck its mark? He wasn't sure because Tanner had dove to one side just as he squeezed off his shot. He wanted to step forward to see for himself if Tanner was fatally wounded, but for some reason he couldn't move. Why did his arms and legs feel so heavy? It took a few seconds for the stinging pain to register. He glanced at his chest to see a deep crimson stain on his shirt. "I—I'm shot," he gasped in startled disbelief.

Zachary's eyes lifted to see Vincent walking slowly toward him, holding a gun. "No!" Zachary cried. "Not you, Vincent! How could you do this to your own father?"

The gun fell from Zachary's hand, and he slumped to his knees, staring up at his son, who now stood directly above him.

* * *

Dodging Zachary's first shot was child's play for Tanner, but just as he prepared to rush the man, a second shot reached his ears. "Vincent?" Tanner whispered loud enough for only himself to hear. "Why didn't you let me handle it?"

Tanner knew from the blood on Zachary's shirt that the bullet had found its mark. He couldn't believe Vincent had actually shot his own father. Not that Tanner wasn't thankful it was over; he was just concerned what this might do to his friend.

Tanner came to his feet just in time to spot Katherine on a dead run toward him. When she reached him, she threw her arms around him and stood there, quivering and saying over and over, "I thought you were shot—I thought you were shot . . ."

Tanner could have said something to comfort her, but he didn't. Instead, he just kept still and enjoyed feeling her in his arms. He wanted to kiss her, and might have done it if she hadn't beat him to it. It wasn't like any kiss they had ever shared before; this one had more meaning. He wished it didn't have to end. As their lips parted, Katherine remained in his arms, sobbing. "It's okay," Tanner said. "Everything's going to be all right."

He didn't know why, but Katherine suddenly pulled away. "I—I'm sorry," she said. "I don't know what got into me."

* * *

"She loves you, Tanner," Mitzi whispered in his ear. "Admit it, you love her too."

"It's no use," Brandon said dejectedly. "It's Tanner's old hang-up about commitment. He can face death and never flinch, but he can't face commitment."

"Never underestimate the power of love," Mitzi countered. "He's hooked, Brandon. Take my word for it."

"I hope you know what you're talking about, Mitzi. But I'll have a hard time believing it until I see him married. We're talking Tanner Nelson here."

"So what are you saying, Brandon? That you just want to give up on this part of the assignment?"

"No, I don't want to give up. It's just that . . ."

"It's just that this part of the assignment is something I'm more qualified to take charge of than you. Just be patient and do what I say. We'll get them together, Brandon, I promise."

* * *

Somehow, Tanner knew this was the moment he had wished for so many times over the years of their separation, but now that it was here, he couldn't bring himself to do a thing about it. All he had to do was say three little words, yet why did those words come so hard? His heart ached watching her now. He knew she was thinking she had made a fool out of herself when in reality he had loved everything about that kiss. She turned and walked toward Vincent, and the moment was gone.

Reaching Zachary's side, Tanner bent down to check the wound. "It's not all that bad," he told Vincent. "I think he's going to live." Tanner then stood to face his friend. "Why'd you shoot him? I had everything under control."

"Yeah, like you always do, but I couldn't take the chance." Vincent glanced down at his father. "This man's DNA may run through my veins, Tanner, but that's as far as it goes. He killed Brandon, he tried to kill you and Katie—what can I say? I've been blind, and I'm so ashamed. I'll see to it that Brandon gets a proper funeral. It's not much, but it's the least I can do."

Tanner dug the chopper keys out of his pocket just as Cory stepped onto the beach, joining the others. "You up to flying that thing home, Vince? Your father does need a doctor."

"Yeah, I'm up to it. Toss me the keys; I'll get it fired up while you and Cory carry him over and strap him in. Don't be too careful with him while you're about it."

"All right, hold it right there! Don't anybody move!"

It was Winston. In the heat of the moment, everyone had forgotten about Winston, who had grabbed the gun Vincent tossed aside after shooting his father. "I'll take those keys now!"

"Put that gun down," Vincent told him. "Shooting people isn't your thing, Winston."

"There's a first time for everything. Give them to me or die on the spot!"

"Look at him, Tanner," Vincent said. "The man hates guns. I doubt he's ever fired one in his life."

Tanner did noticed a slight tremor in Winston's hand, but the man's eyes told a different story. He was a killer at heart. The question was, could Tanner press Winston into doing something stupid? "Toss the keys into the ocean," Tanner calmly told Vincent.

"No!" Winston snapped. "Try it and you die!"

"You better take a look around, Winston," Tanner spoke up. "I'm on your left, Vincent's on your right, and Cory is at your back. You might get one of us; with luck you might even get two. But you can't get all three. You're not that fast. Give it up, Winston, while you still can."

"Shut up! No more of your little games, Tanner. I'm not blind. I know how you feel about this woman. Anything you try—anything at all—and the first shot hits her heart. Now, throw those keys over here, Vincent!"

"Throw them in the ocean, Vince," Tanner said. "He's going to kill us anyway. Why give him a way out?"

"Stop it, Winston," Zachary said, his voice strained and barely audible. "I have money hidden away . . ." He swallowed and grimaced in pain before going on. "I have enough for the two of us to live in luxury the rest of our lives. Listen to what I'm saying, Winston. Kill the others. Drop Vincent off someplace where he'll be safe. The two of us can simply disappear."

Winston hurled a kick at Zachary, causing him to double over in pain. Even as a weakened moan escaped his lips, Zachary noticed the gun he himself had dropped lying only inches from his face.

"The keys!" Winston demanded again. "You've got thirty seconds before I blast the girl!" Katherine was standing only feet away from Winston. Tanner knew Winston couldn't miss at this range.

Unnoticed by all but Tanner, who happened to glance down, Zachary quietly reached for the gun, which still held two shots. Tanner slowly moved his foot between Zachary's hand and the gun. Zachary looked up, and their eyes yet. There was a pleading in Zachary's eyes, an appeal that Tanner understood. Tanner gave a slight nod and moved his foot.

"I warned you," Winston said, the gun still aimed at Katherine. "Time's up!"

The sound of Zachary's shot echoed in the air. Winston let out a groan and slumped to the sand.

Zachary moved the gun around and pointed it at his own head. "No, Father!" Vincent cried. "That's not the way!"

Tanner pulled Katherine behind him and watched as Vincent fell to one knee beside his father. "Don't, Father, please."

Zachary's voice was only a coarse whisper now. "Try to understand, son. I've lost everything. I can't live in a prison cell. This is the way I want it."

"You say you love me! If you do this, I'll never forgive myself. Is that what you want, to give me a lifetime of pain and guilt I can never overcome?" There was a long moment of silence as the two looked at each other. "I'll visit you, I promise," Vincent said.

Vincent closed his eyes just before the gun went off. "No!" he screamed. He felt a hand on his shoulder. Opening his eyes, he saw that it was Tanner. "It's okay," Tanner said. "Winston wasn't dead. Your father finished him just as he was about to get off a shot."

Vincent gazed at his father, who was still very much alive. No words passed between them. Tanner checked Winston and found no pulse. He swallowed, then spoke to Vincent. "You know what they say—all for one and one for all. I'm sorry I ever doubted you, old friend."

"I'm so sorry too," Katherine said, leaning down next to Vincent. "I know how much you love your father."

"Ditto for the disc jockey," Cory added. "Still friends?"

* * *

"I hope that's the last of them," Brandon remarked as he and Mitzi watched Gabe escort Winston away. "I know one thing for sure—I don't ever want a job in Gabe's department." Brandon reached out and touched Mitzi's cheek. "No way could I have ever gotten through this assignment without your help," he told her. "Thanks."

"It's not over yet," Mitzi reminded him. "I have some match-making to do, remember?"

CHAPTER 28

Troy Adams lay on his cell bunk reading an article from a magazine. He glanced up to see the familiar face of Buddy Marshall grinning at him through the bars. Buddy was one of the prison guards, one who had taken a liking to Troy. "It's your lucky day, Adams," Buddy quipped as he unlocked the cell. "Proctor wants to see you."

"The warden?" Troy responded, tossing the magazine aside. "What's he want with me?"

"He's pulling you off kitchen duty and assigning you to latrine detail," Buddy said, rolling his eyes. "How am I supposed to know what the warden wants? But the man was wearing a smile when he ordered me to bring you in. That should count for something."

Troy stepped out of the cell, and Buddy closed the door behind him. Together, they moved down the hall past several other cells. "What did Mr. Adams do to get himself called to the warden's office?" Hank Forbs, one of the inmates, piped up. Hank was nicknamed Chatter Mouth for good reason. He always had something to say, and it was seldom anything of consequence.

"Put a cork in it," Buddy remarked without even giving Hank the satisfaction of a look in his direction. "You wouldn't like it if your mail just happened to get misplaced for the next couple of weeks."

"Mail?" Hank retorted with a burst of gruff laughter. "Who's gonna write me? Kiss old Proctor's cheek for me while yer in there, Adams. And ask him what he's heard about my pardon."

"Ignore him," Buddy said, soft enough that only Troy could hear. "It's the worst thing you can do to Hank. He hates it when his mouth fails to get him the attention he craves."

Troy only smiled. Who could ever ignore Hank? Even Buddy had responded to his first remark. Hank was harmless, and he added a little color to the normally gray world belonging to those in the confines of this place.

They reached the secondary security gate, and it swung open. It was a strange feeling for Troy. The only time he ever saw this gate open was when the whole bunch from his block were ushered through it at once. It looked so much bigger this way, and he half expected to hear a siren blare as he stepped through it. This brought a laugh, thinking about what prison life had done to him. He used to have thoughts and dreams of a life on the outside again. But as time went by, those things had mercifully faded into oblivion, allowing him to maintain his sanity. Dwelling on what might have been would have ripped his heart out.

Those first two grueling years had been the worst. He was so embittered by anger back then, sure that even God had forgotten him, and he lashed out venomously at a system that would do this to him. He was innocent, but no one would listen. Appeal after useless appeal fell on deaf ears. It didn't seem to matter that the evidence convicting him was paper-thin and that there were no witnesses, no apparent motive, not even a body. All that seemed to matter was the point of view of an ambitious prosecution lawyer who refused to admit he might have twisted a few facts to prove his case. But Troy had come to realize that was just the way Rowan Kentwood operated. Once the man put someone away, it became his goal to keep them there forever, regardless of what new evidence might be uncovered.

The bitterness of those first two years had nearly destroyed Troy. But thanks to his strong belief in the power of prayer, he had at last found the courage to turn things around. Little by little, he picked up the pieces and got back into the game of moving on. Not that prison ever became enjoyable—that could never happen. But once the bitterness had subsided, Troy realized God hadn't really forsaken him at all. Even here in this tiny cell, there was still rich meaning to his life. Self-pity was replaced by newfound ambition. Troy set his sights on what seemed to most an unattainable goal. It took four and a half years of grueling work, but he earned his law degree from right within the confines of his own cell. And he didn't let the degree go to waste.

He had now helped three fellow prisoners secure an early release by convincing the parole board they were ready.

"Come in, young man," Allan Proctor said as Buddy and Troy arrived at his office. "And relax, you're not here because of anything bad." Troy hadn't known of any negative reason for the warden wanting to see him, but having it verified did bring a degree of relief.

"Will you be needing me any longer, Warden?" Buddy asked.

"No, Buddy, that'll be all for now." Proctor pointed to a chair in front of his desk. "Have a seat, Troy."

As Troy sat down, he noticed the warden had been holding a document, which he now laid aside. "I'm really proud of you, Troy," the warden said. "You've become one of our model prisoners. Truth be known, you've become *the* model prisoner in our ranks. If all my inmates here were half as cooperative as you, my job would be a snap." Proctor picked up a pencil, then, leaning back in his chair, he rolled it between his forefinger and thumb. "The reason I've asked you here," he continued, "is to tell you you're being moved to another facility."

Troy wasn't sure he had heard right. "Another facility?" he echoed.

"I'm not at liberty to give you all the details just yet—for security reasons, you know. But I can tell you that this transfer comes by order of the governor."

"The governor? What could the governor possibly care about me, Warden?"

"Sorry, Troy, no details for now. You'll just have to be patient. Now, listen to what I'm about to tell you. When it comes to transporting prisoners outside these walls, I have a few rules. In your case I could overlook these rules, but that wouldn't be setting the best precedent. You can see my point, can't you, Troy?"

"Yes, sir."

"Good, then here are my rules, all three of them. Handcuffs, leg cuffs, and a blindfold. That about covers it unless you have questions."

"Just one, Warden. What about my personal things? In my cell?"

"I'll see to your personal items myself. You have my word I'll get them all securely back into your hands."

Both men stood, and the warden offered his hand. Troy readily accepted the handshake, but it certainly felt strange. In all his dealings with the warden, there had never been a handshake. "Good luck,"

Proctor said. "And hang on tight to that good attitude of yours. It'll take you a long way, wherever you may end up."

Troy felt a curious sadness realizing this could be the last he'd ever see of Allan Proctor. Why should he care? Proctor was just a warden in a prison where Troy didn't belong in the first place. But, strangely, he did care. "I know you probably hear this from all your guests, Warden, but in my case it's true. I didn't kill Brandon Cheney."

"I know that, Troy. I've known it all along."

The warden's response couldn't have caught Troy more off guard. "Thanks," was all he managed to say.

The warden pressed a button on his desk, and two guards entered the room. "Take good care of this man," the warden directed. "And don't snap the cuffs any tighter than necessary."

CHAPTER 29

Try as he might, Troy could make no sense of any of this. What interest could the governor possibly have in him? Where were they transporting him, and why was it taking so long to get there? With the blindfold on, he couldn't see a clock in the car or even the position of the sun, but he estimated they'd been on the road no less than three hours by the time the car made its final stop. The door next to him opened, and he got a sudden whiff of pines. Did Arizona have a new prison facility in the mountains? Not that he'd heard of. He felt an arm on his shoulder, and the guard's voice was the first he had heard since being driven away from the prison. "Just relax, Troy. Step out and lean on me. I'm not permitted to remove the blindfold just yet, so I'll have to be your eyes for now."

Troy felt the guard release the snap on his seat belt. Moving his legs around, he exited the car and allowed the guard to lead him away from it. "There's five steps right in front of you," the guard said. "Just take them one at a time and you'll be all right."

Troy counted the steps as he climbed them and then stopped. "What's going on?" he asked.

"We're here," the guard responded. "I suppose you'd like those cuffs off about now, eh?"

"What do you think?" Troy laughed. "I've just ridden three hours with these things biting at my ankles and wrists. Yeah, I want them off."

Troy could swear he heard the fellow stifle a laugh. "It was only two and a half hours," he said as he removed the cuffs, giving Troy back the use of his arms. The leg cuffs were removed next. "Okay," the guard said. "You can take that thing off your eyes."

Troy pulled it away and blinked three or four times as his eyes adjusted to the light. Within moments he found himself staring at a giant banner with the words *Welcome Home, Troy* printed in bold red letters. "What the . . . ?" he gasped, realizing he was on the doorstep of Zachary Wagner's mountain cabin. "Why have you brought me here?"

Troy's only answer was applause, cheers, whistles, and scattered shouts of "Way to go, buddy!" Somewhere in the background, a trumpet blared a loud, off-key note.

Glancing through the open door before him, he saw hordes of people all smiling at him. Some had tears in their eyes. Tanner was there, as well as Vincent and Cory. Troy could hardly contain himself when he spotted Katherine. There were so many others; it was impossible to count them all. "What is this?" he choked out. "Am I dreaming?"

Tanner, Vincent, and Cory all reached him at the same time. There were so many shoulder punches and back slaps Troy thought he might be bowled over. "If I am a dream," Cory shouted in his face, "I'm the ugliest dream you'll ever wake from. Welcome home, buddy!"

"You never did pay up that five bucks you owe me," Tanner chided. "Don't think I've forgotten it either."

Vincent grabbed Troy by the arm and led him inside the room. "Don't pay any attention to Tanner," he said. "I'll make good the five bucks myself. Right now we have some partying to do, and since you're the guest of honor, you have to make a speech."

Troy's head was spinning. "Is this still your father's cabin?" he asked.

"Actually, it's my cabin now, but that's a story you've yet to hear. What better place to celebrate your first day of freedom than the place your celebrated your last? The graduation party, remember?"

Troy stopped in his tracks and stared at Vincent. "My first day of freedom?" he said weakly. "What are you saying, Vince?"

"He's saying the governor signed your pardon," came a familiar voice from behind. Troy turned to see Warden Allan Proctor. "Remember that document I was holding when you came in my office?" the warden asked. "It was your pardon, Troy." Proctor handed Troy the paper.

"I—I've been pardoned?" he asked in disbelief, staring at the document.

"Yes, you have," the warden assured. "And you should see what Rowan Kentwood looks like with a mouthful of crow feathers. He's been on every news channel and the front page of every newspaper in the valley. He's the laughingstock of the town, Troy, and well he should be. Oh, and by the way, I'd like to clear the air on one thing. The cuffs and blindfold weren't really my idea. You have three very special friends—I think you can guess who they are—who insisted on that part. I was the one who chauffeured you here, though. I hope it was a smooth enough ride. I gave it my best."

Troy still couldn't make himself believe this was real. "But how could I have been pardoned?" he asked. "With no new evidence to support my case?"

The warden laughed. "Enjoy the party, Troy. There'll be time enough to hear about the new evidence after you've finished all the cake you can eat."

"Enough of this," Vincent said, pushing Troy forward again. "We want a speech!"

Suddenly Troy found himself in front of a mike, staring out over the throng of well-wishers. The whole room instantly turned silent. Troy swallowed and let his eyes slowly scan the roomful of people staring back at him. "I, uh, don't really know what to say," he stammered. "This is Cory Harper's sort of thing, not mine."

"He's right!" Cory yelled out. "Enough of his jabbering. Let's party!" Cory started clapping. A moment later, Tanner joined in, then Vincent. Soon the whole room exploded in another round of roaring applause.

Troy's heart leapt as he spotted Katherine walking his way. He had no idea what she was up to until she planted a kiss right on his lips. "That's my welcome home," she told him as the applause grew even louder. "The guys have laid out some clothes for you in one of the bedrooms upstairs—the one with a big red X on the door. Go get changed and I'll save you a dance."

Halfway up the stairs, Troy paused to look out over the party that was now in full swing below him. This had to be one of two things. Either it was his happiest dream ever or it was the happiest day of his life. He still wasn't sure which.

* * *

Mitzi brushed aside a tear. "You did yourself proud, Brandon," she sniffled. "You can put one more part of your assignment in the file drawer. And let me thank you again for allowing me to be part of it."

"Having you along for the ride was my pleasure, believe me, Mitzi. And I learned a bunch about this guardian angel thing along the way. I have to say, it's more fun than the records department."

"Ever think about requesting a transfer?"

"Can I do that?"

"Of course you can. It's done all the time. Angels have rights."

"We do? I mean, of course we do. I think I'll speak to my supervisor tomorrow."

Mitzi beamed at thoughts of Brandon working in her department. Maybe she could pull some strings to get him assigned to her district. It was something to think about.

"So?" Brandon asked with just a hint of sadness in his voice after looking around at all his friends one last time. "Are you ready to report back in and call this assignment done?"

Mitzi shook her head. "I haven't finished yet," she said.

"Mitzi, be realistic. Tanner is a lost cause in the romance department. He has completely shied away from Katherine since she kissed him on the island two days ago. The rest of my assignment was a success. Why not let it end on that note?"

"No deal, Brandon," Mitzi said, seeing Katherine on one side of the room and Tanner on the opposite. "Come on, we have work to do."

* * *

Katherine watched Troy climb the stairs and disappear down the hall at the top. She almost wished she hadn't said she'd save him a dance. Not that she wasn't happy to see him, but all she really wanted to do was get as far away from this party and Tanner Nelson as possible. She had made a fool out of herself over him for the last time. What wasn't meant to be just wasn't meant to be—even if it meant a broken heart.

She had already made arrangements to vacate his apartment just as soon as her new apartment came available in a day or two. Staying away from him while living in the room next door might not prove all that easy, although he hadn't done one thing to bother her since returning from the island where all the excitement had happened. Why had she ever kissed him like that? It was stupid. She'd never do it again, and that she knew for sure.

So why did she keep hearing this little voice telling her to go over and talk with him now? There was no way she was about to listen. Still, it was a tempting idea. What could it hurt, just telling him good-bye one last time? She wouldn't have to get mushy or anything. She could just keep it businesslike.

"No! I won't do it!" Katherine suddenly blurted out without even thinking who might be listening. She felt instantly like a fool when she realized Cory had just stepped up.

"Won't do what?" Cory asked.

"Uh, nothing," she excused. "I don't know why I said that."

"You want to dance?"

Katherine tried to laugh. "You sure your wife won't mind?"

"How can she when she's over there dancing with Tanner?"

Katherine looked to see Tanner and Stephanie in the center of the dance floor. She felt Cory take her hand and allowed him to lead her onto the dance floor.

"So," Cory said, making small talk, "what do you think of Vince? You know, the way he's taking this thing about learning what kind of man his dad really is?"

"I'd say he's taking it pretty well," Katherine answered. "I've never seen a man more devoted to his father than Vincent. It must have been a terrible blow when he was forced to face the truth."

"Yeah, and in a strange way, the old man is nuts about Vincent. I, for one, am glad he's been exposed. Vincent's better off that way."

"I think Vincent knows that now, Cory, but he's still a dedicated son. He's trying to get a plea bargain worked out for Zachary to plead guilty to murder on all counts in order to avoid the death penalty."

"I guess that's a good thing," Cory conceded. "Vince doesn't condone what his father did, and he's doing everything he can to make things right with Wagner Aerospace. I guess not completely turning his back on the old man is commendable. Personally, I'd like to see the guy fry, but I'm betting if Brandon had any input, he'd go along with Vince."

"Somehow I know you're right about that, Cory." Katherine was about to say something else but was cut short when Cory managed to push her into another dancer. "I'm sorry," she said even before turning to see who it was. When she did look, it brought a gasp. Tanner. Cory had done it on purpose. Boy was he in trouble when she got him alone.

"Wow, Tanner," Cory commented. "Who's this looker you're dancing with? Mind if I cut in?"

Tanner stepped aside, and Cory hurriedly swept his wife away. After a long, awkward moment, Tanner bit the bullet and asked, "You want to dance or something?"

Katherine didn't know where the courage came from, but for once in her life she faced the problem of Tanner Nelson straight on. "No, I don't want to dance. I want to talk. Can we step out onto the patio?"

Tanner looked surprised, but she didn't care. "All right," he said. Then, taking her by the hand, he led her through the double doors and to a remote corner of the patio. "Will this do?" he asked.

"Yes," she responded.

"So, uh, what do you want to talk about?"

The little voice in her head had become increasingly insistent that she tell him exactly what was on her mind. She knew what that was, and she was past the point of sidestepping it. "Let me ask you a question," she began. "That morning at the restaurant, you know, before I left for Australia . . ." She paused, giving him time to catch up.

"At Denny's?" he responded. "What about it?"

She continued quickly before she lost her courage. "You had a ring in your pocket. I want to know, Tanner Nelson, was that really meant for a joke—or had you intended to propose that morning?"

Tanner nearly choked. Composing himself, he leaned against the railing with his hands cupped in front of him and his head lowered. "It wasn't a joke," he said.

"Then why didn't you do it?"

"Because . . ."

"Because why?"

"Because you would have turned me down."

"You don't know that! You didn't give me a chance to respond!"

"You were moving to Australia, Katie. And you didn't bother telling me until just hours before your flight."

"What does that have to do with anything? So I was moving to Australia. Would that have stopped me from saying *yes?*"

Tanner managed a laugh. "You were there eight years. That sounds like a long engagement by any stretch of the imagination."

"I was there eight years because I was afraid to come home. I had no idea what I'd find. You refused to answer my letters, and you never called even once." Her voice took on a hurt tone. "Why didn't you answer my letters? I want to at least know that."

"I didn't answer your letters because I didn't want to interfere in your new life. I didn't want you to feel tied down to me."

Katherine stepped up behind Tanner, and he twisted around just enough to show his face without actually looking at her. "Are you saying if I had proposed, you might not have stayed eight years in Australia?"

Her voice dropped a level. "That's exactly what I'm saying. I might have stayed six months, maybe even eight. Just long enough to be sure my folks were going to be okay. Then I would have come home."

"What about your teaching job?"

"Okay, I might have ended up teaching one year, but then I would have come home." Katherine moved around next to him, forcing him to straighten and face her. "You know what I think?" she said. "I think you knew I'd come home if you proposed to me. I think you used my going to Australia as an excuse *not* to propose. I have no idea how our relationship ever got as far as you buying a ring, but with your aversion to commitment, I'm betting you were looking for a way out. If it hadn't been for my going to Australia, it would have been something else."

"That's not true! I don't have an aversion to commitment!"

"Ha!"

"And I *was* going to propose that night!"

"Double ha!"

Katherine was floored as she watched Tanner dig a little black box out of his pocket, one that looked exactly like the one from that night. "What is that?" she gasped.

"It's the ring," he admitted.

"The same one?"

"Yeah, the same one. I nearly broke the bank to buy this thing back then. I wasn't about to get rid of it."

Katherine felt her heart race as she looked at the little black box. "Why did you bring it here today?" she asked.

Tanner turned back to face the garden. "I don't know."

"You brought it with the idea of asking me to marry you right here at this party! Am I right?"

"I suppose I did."

Katherine waited for something else besides *I suppose I did,* but Tanner just stood there looking off into the sunny afternoon sky.

"Oh, I get it," she said at length. "You were looking for another way out, and this discussion was all it took. More aversion to commitment."

Katherine was crying, but she couldn't help it. If she thought Tanner Nelson would ever come around to the point of proposing, she was just kidding herself. He wasn't the marrying kind. Never had been, and never would be. Well, this would be the last chance he'd ever have to break her heart. She straightened and stared at him. "I'm going to tell you something, Tanner Nelson. You see those doors right over there?" She pointed to the doors leading back inside the cabin. "I'm going to turn around, and I'm going to walk right through them. You have until I take one step inside to make up your mind. If I make it that far without hearing a certain question from your lips, you'll never get the chance to ask it again. You think about that."

Katherine drew a deep breath, turned to face the doors, and took a slow step forward. She closed her eyes and hoped to feel his hand on her shoulder. Nothing. She took another step and paused. Still nothing. Not the touch of his hand, not one sound from his lips. She took another step, then another. She opened her eyes to see the doors looming in front of her. What had she done? Putting Tanner on the spot like this was pure insanity. But she had declared her word, and backing down wasn't an option. She inched her way toward the door, reaching it only after what seemed like an eternity. She wanted to look back, but there was no looking back now. Hot tears flooded onto her cheeks as she grabbed the knob and pulled the door open. "Good-bye, Tanner," she whispered. "I hope you find whatever it is you're looking for." She drew another breath and started to step through the opening.

"Everyone, I want your attention!"

What was that? It came from the loudspeakers, and it sounded like . . .

Katherine moved a step forward where she could see the stage. "What . . . ?" she choked over her tears. "How did he . . . ?"

It was Tanner. He had somehow gotten past her, and he was standing at the stage holding the mike. How had he done it? "Impossible for anyone but Tanner Nelson," she quietly sobbed to herself.

"I have something I want everyone in the room to hear," Tanner said into the mike. "My only regret is that there aren't television cameras carrying it to the rest of Arizona."

Katherine could only stare through watery eyes. Tanner removed the black box again, this time opening it. "I have something here," he said. "It's for the most beautiful woman in the world, if she'll take it. I've seen a lot of this world, so I figure that qualifies me to know she's the most beautiful."

"What are you doing?" Katherine called to him. "Are you trying to propose?"

A hush filled the room as all eyes shifted back to Tanner. "Will you have me, Katie?" he asked.

"I don't know!" she sobbed. "Why do you want to marry me?"

"Because you're beautiful . . ."

"Why else?"

"Because you're Katie Dalton."

"That's not good enough. Why else do you want to marry me?"

"Because he loves you, Katie!" Vincent called out, drawing a laugh from the crowd. "And because you love him too. Tell the man *yes* so we can get on with the party!"

"I want to hear it from him. Why do you want to marry me, Tanner Nelson?"

Tanner shoved the mike back in the holder and started toward Katherine. She was crying and laughing at the same time as he approached her. He stopped only inches away. "Because I love you, Katie Dalton. And because I can't stand the thought of living one more day without you." He lifted her hand to slide on the ring. "Now, will you marry me?"

Katherine threw her arms around him as the sound of Beethoven's Ninth Symphony filled the room. She wasn't sure whether it came from the band or just from her heart, but it didn't matter. Their lips met, and suddenly her world became more beautiful than all the symphonies ever written.

* * *

"You did it, Mitzi," Brandon cried. "I don't know how, but you did it!"

"Yes," Mitzi sniffed. "Talk about a three-tissue-box ending. Have you ever seen anything more beautiful in your life, Brandon?"

"No, can't say that I have. Not in life as a mortal or as an angel." He stepped around to face her. "Too bad Tanner was wrong."

"What?"

"About him getting the most beautiful woman. He only got second-best."

Mitzi wiped an eye and looked back at Brandon. "Who's the first?" she asked.

"A certain angel I know." He beamed. "How would you like to go to dinner with me? I know this great place called the Paradise Palace. They have a chef there, Jason Hackett I think his name is. Talk about out-of-this-world dining."

Mitzi couldn't get her *yes* out fast enough. To think that Brandon thought she was beautiful! Life as an angel was always good, but never quite as good as at this very moment. Slipping her arm through his, she allowed him to escort her through the luminous door that opened to take them home to the world of angels.

ABOUT THE AUTHOR

Since grade school, Dan's been busy putting words on paper in one capacity or another. It's been the love of his life. His first novel, *Angels Don't Knock,* was published in 1994. *Walk with an Angel* is his eleventh novel, and he hopes to keep writing for many years to come.

Dan lives in Phoenix with his wife, Shelby. They have six children and twenty-one grandchildren whose names all appear somewhere within the pages of his novels. Dan has served in many capacities in the Church and has been a bishop twice and a high counselor four times. He now teaches the fourteen- and fifteen-year-olds in Sunday School, and he says this calling is one of the most fulfilling and challenging he's ever had.

Dan also filled one term on the Riverside County School Board in California and has been involved in other community services as well. Dan loves hearing from his readers, and they can reach him by e-mailing info@covenant-lds.com.